Thomas E Taylor

Running the Blockade

Thomas E Taylor

Running the Blockade

ISBN/EAN: 9783337375478

Printed in Europe, USA, Canada, Australia, Japan

Cover: Foto ©Andreas Hilbeck / pixelio.de

More available books at **www.hansebooks.com**

RUNNING THE BLOCKADE

A PERSONAL NARRATIVE OF ADVENTURES, RISKS, AND ESCAPES DURING THE AMERICAN CIVIL WAR

By THOMAS E. TAYLOR

WITH AN INTRODUCTION BY JULIAN CORBETT
MAPS AND ILLUSTRATIONS

LONDON
JOHN MURRAY, ALBEMARLE STREET
1896

INTRODUCTION

A GERMAN admiral has remarked that the most
valuable naval history lies in the despatches
and logs of naval officers. Our own Navy
Record Society by the line it has taken
thoroughly endorses this view, and has com-
mitted itself to the teaching of naval history
from the mouths of the men who made it.

Mr. Taylor's work then must not be taken
as a mere record of personal adventure, however absorbing it be found from this point of
view. As a picture of exciting escapes, of
coolness and resource at moments of acute
danger, of well-calculated risks, boldly accepted
and obstinately carried through, it has few
rivals in recent sea-story : but its deeper value
does not lie here. Over and above its
romantic interest it will be recognised by
students of the naval art as a real and solid
contribution to history ; for it presents to us

from the pen of a principal actor the most
complete account we have of a great blockade
in the days of steam.

The important part that blockade plays in
naval warfare is a thing hardly recognised
outside professional ranks. For the general
reader, the grand manœuvres of a great fleet
in chase of the enemy and the stirring hours
of some decisive action throw into oblivion
the tedious months of dull, anxious, and ex-
hausting work with which by far the greater
part of the war is taken up. Yet it is hardly
too much to say that during the most glorious
period of our maritime history nine-tenths of
the energies of our admirals were devoted to
blockade. In the future it is possible that
it will take even a higher place. Should
England become engaged with a first-rate
foreign power, single-handed, it is a recognised
fact amongst naval strategists that in a week
she could close every one of her enemy's ports
and have a fleet free to reduce at its leisure
everything he held beyond the seas. With
almost any two Powers against her it is probable she could do as much : and it is the

recognition of this power abroad which gives England, in spite of her military weakness, so commanding a position in Europe.

The importance then of studying every scrap of information on the subject in order to perfect our knowledge of the art of blockade cannot be exaggerated, and Mr. Taylor's simple and straightforward record of his experiences may claim to be perhaps the fullest contribution to the subject that as yet exists. Experiences of individual captains we have had, and, read with the present work, they are of high value : but Mr. Taylor has something more to tell. Not only did he run the blockade personally a greater number of times than any one else, but, boy as he was at the time, he was the chief organiser of a great and systematised attack on the Northern blockade, such as the world had never seen before. His operations may be said to have opened a new era in the history of blockade, and one which bids fair to have far-reaching consequences for every maritime Power.

To make clear his position and its dangers and difficulties a word must be said on the general subject of blockade. Blockade, it must be clearly borne in mind, is of two kinds, the one military, the other commercial. The first concerns the belligerents alone, and consists in one of them, who has obtained a working command of the sea, imprisoning the other's war fleets in their own ports. It was this form of blockade which absorbed by far the greatest part of our naval activity during the great French wars. During the American Civil War it was considerably practised, and from American sources may be studied in complete detail the efforts of the Confederate war-ships to escape the vigilance of Federal blockading squadrons. The second form, or commercial blockade, is one that principally concerns neutrals, and it was of course to this form alone that Mr. Taylor's operations extended.

The International Law which regulates its conditions as between neutrals and belligerents is shortly this. A belligerent, if strong enough at sea to close one or more ports of his enemy, may give notice to Neutral Powers that such port or ports are blockaded, and thereafter if

any neutral vessel attempts to enter or leave
them, the belligerent may treat it as an enemy,
and may destroy or capture and condemn it as
an ordinary prize. To run a blockade then is
an operation attended with all the risks of war.
Indeed a blockade-runner is in an even worse
position than a hostile belligerent ; for not being
a combatant he may not resist the efforts of the
blockaders to destroy or capture him. He is
entitled to escape if he can, but a single shot
or blow in his own defence makes him a pirate,
and a belligerent capturing him may treat him
as such. But it must always be remembered
that for a belligerent to be entitled to exercise
these high prerogatives he must first have
constituted a real and effective blockade. A
mere declaration that a port is closed is
not enough. It must be so closely watched
and invested with an adequate naval force
that no neutral can leave or enter without running present danger of being sunk or
captured.

Analogous to the rights arising out of an
effective blockade, and always to be clearly
distinguished from them, is the right of a

b

belligerent to treat as an enemy a neutral vessel carrying contraband of war to his enemy's ports, and this right he may always exercise, whether the ports in question be effectively blockaded or not.

It was this consideration, no doubt, combined with a desire to preserve a strict neutrality and to see the South treated as belligerents and not as mere insurgents, that induced the English Government to recognise the Federal blockade as soon as it was declared. At the opening of the war the Federal Government, in defiance of International Law, declared the whole Southern seaboard under blockade. It was a blockade they were then wholly unable to enforce or even to pretend to enforce, but as most of our blockade-runners carried contraband of war, there was very little to be gained by disputing the Federal pretensions. Some injustice, no doubt, was thus done to the South. But it was more than counterbalanced by the advantage they gained in that the recognition of the blockade made them indisputably belligerents. For these reasons our Government thought it wise to waive its neutral rights and submit to a paper blockade, which did not exist. As the Northern power increased at sea the blockade became more and more effective, and by the time Mr. Taylor had got fully to work it may be said to have been something more than a pretence. Finally it became very strict and thoroughly effective, and it is with this instructive period that his reminiscences are chiefly concerned.

This declaration of a blockade that could not be enforced at the time was not the only extension of belligerent rights which the Federal Government claimed and exercised in respect of blockade. As Mr. Taylor fully explains, they did not confine their operations against blockade-runners to the established practice of watching the closed ports. Not only did they cruise for offenders on the high seas, but they intercepted them close to their points of departure, thousands of miles from the blockaded ports. Nay, they even went so far as to attempt to blockade the neutral ports which the offending vessels were using as bases of operations. To most of these claims no objection was made, and there is no doubt that in any future war similar operations will be recognised without question, as within belligerent rights.

In previous wars a belligerent declaring a blockade had to concern himself with little more than turning back ordinary merchantmen who had not received notice of the blockade, or cutting off small fry of the smuggling type that slipped over from adjacent coasts to take their chance of getting in. Such a thing as neutral merchants establishing public companies to build fleets of specially designed vessels for the avowed purpose of breaking a blockade which was thoroughly effective against ordinary types of merchantmen, was a thing unknown to International Law. And further, when these merchants stretched their rights as neutrals so far as to establish regular bases almost in the enemy's waters from which to conduct their revolutionary operations, it was obvious that some latitude must be granted to the block-ading power. No objection, therefore, was ever raised to his cutting off vessels avowedly constructed for blockade-running at any point he chose; but when he attempted to blockade neutral ports from which they were acting,

England put her foot down and compelled the
Federal cruisers to draw off. In this she was
clearly within her rights. But although the
Federal claim to this bold extension of belligerent rights was undoubtedly illegal, it was
not without provocation. It is another law
of blockade that a vessel is not "guilty" and
cannot be interfered with unless it is bound for
a blockaded port. The system pursued by
Mr. Taylor of establishing depots or bases on
British territory close to American waters thus
greatly increased the difficulties of the cruisers.
Goods destined for the blockaded ports were
consigned first to one of these bases, Bermuda,
Havana, or the Bahamas, and on their way could
not be touched by the Northern captains. It
was naturally a great temptation to these officers
as they watched the offensive traffic pouring into
the runner's bases to see that it did not get
out. It is even conceivable that England
might have been induced to wink at their pro-
ceedings. But it so happened that the first and
only attempt to blockade blockade-runners in a
British port was made by the very officer who
was the culprit in the *Trent* affair, and that too

while we were still unsoothed from his last vio-
lation of our neutrality. The British Government, therefore, happened to be in a very
irritable mood with the North, and though
they had hitherto been inexhaustible in their
sympathy with the Federal belligerent pretensions, they now peremptorily stopped their
complacency and the North had to submit.

Whether the claim made tentatively by
the Northern Government is destined to
become recognised by International Law is
by no means clear. In the case in question
the neutral was too powerful to be resisted.
Shortly after, however, the same scheme was
actually put in operation by one of the most
famous of Mr. Taylor's colleagues, the
"notorious Captain Roberts," the arch-blockade
runner and a British naval officer. When
the American war closed, the Turkish Government had been trying for months to suppress
an insurrection in Crete by blockading the
island on the old lines. Hobart (whose *nom
de guerre* as a blockade-runner was "Roberts"),
profiting by his recent experience, undertook
to suppress it in a week, and his offer was

accepted. The insurgents were living entirely on supplies sent them from Greece, and Hobart having been placed in command of the blockading squadron proceeded at once to blockade the Greek vessels in their own ports, and the Cretans were immediately starved into surrender.

This and every other indication show a tendency for the belligerent rights of blockade to increase at the expense of the neutral. If this be so, then blockade must become a more and more effective naval operation, and hence the importance of its study down to the minutest particulars from which any forecast of the future may be obtained.

For the non-professional reader one of the chief points of technical interest in Mr. Taylor's book will be the light it throws on a great national question, which periodically comes out in moments of alarm. It is now a common subject for paragraphists to dilate upon how, if England lost command of the sea, her food supply would be cut off in a week (or some other minute period) and herself be brought to the mercy of her enemy. However useful such prognostications may be for stimulating an interest in the navy, they are full of fallacies and even dangerous as leading to demands for naval armaments so extravagant as to cause the taxpayer to turn his back on the navy altogether, and button his pockets in sheer disgust. To begin with, if England lost the command of the sea, it does not follow that any one else would obtain it, a fact too often lost sight of in naval discussion. The thing does not hang in a simple dilemma. You cannot say, either England has the command or her enemy has it. There is still the middle hypothesis, that neither has it. And this in all reasonable probability is the worst that could suddenly befall us. The destruction of England's command of the sea is no child's play, and even if three Powers together succeeded in doing it, it could only be at such a sacrifice to themselves as would leave the seas practically free to the operations of neutrals. Mr. Taylor's experiences show clearly how surprisingly easy it was for bold and expert captains with adequate vessels to run the most strict and effective blockades.

Were England to become engaged in a great war, the first step would be for numbers of her mercantile marine to pass to neutral flags, and all these vessels with their crews would be ready-made blockade-runners the moment there was a call for them. And even assuming that by some extraordinary chance the British fleet for a time was suppressed with little or no damage to the enemy, the precedents of the American war go to show that the navies of three Powers absolutely intact could hardly avail to maintain a blockade of such a coast-line as ours.

The conditions of blockade, it is true, have changed, but the balance remains much the same. Mr. Taylor considers that search-lights, for instance, tell quite as much for one side as the other. Increased speed is at least as favourable for running as it is for blockading. Torpedo boats seem hardly to affect the balance at all. For while they render the position of a blockading squadron less secure than formerly, they on the other hand furnish it with ideal patrols. Quick-firing guns are all in favour of the blockader, but on the other hand, long-range guns of position are all against him, compelling him to keep further to sea and so to cover more ground. The extreme importance of invisibility too, on which Mr. Taylor insists, shows how great an advantage a runner, able to procure good smokeless coal, would have over a force blockading the English coast which could not obtain it. On the whole we may safely conclude that a commercial blockade is certainly no easier than it was in the sixties. Many indications from the following pages show how difficult it is to maintain the blockade even of half a dozen ports, if you are unable to intercept the regular runners at their points of departure. This a force without undisputed mastery of the sea could never effect to a sufficient extent. The lesson then that the following pages most clearly teaches is, that the danger of the British Isles being blockaded by any conceivable combination of hostile Powers, so as to reduce her even approximately near starvation, may be dismissed as outside the region of practical strategy; and in the next place they show us the vast importance of maintaining in our navy an adequate force of vessels of a type calculated to render a commercial blockade really effective. What Mr. Taylor was able to do with one little steamer to prolong Lee's resistance is a lesson to be remembered beside Dundonald's operations on the coast of Spain.

Such are a few of the considerations which Mr. Taylor's book suggests. Different men will draw different lessons from the facts it presents, but its value as the work of a man of unequalled experience in the working of a great blockade will be admitted by all: and whatever weight may be attached to the author's conclusions from his practical experience, the little work will amply justify its existence if it in any way stimulates interest in the practical side of a subject, which naval writers seem inclined to leave too much in the hands of International lawyers.

JULIAN CORBETT.

May 1896.

CONTENTS

CHAPTER VII

ILLUSTRATIONS, MAPS, Etc.

CHAPTER I

HOW I BEGAN

AT the outbreak of the great American Civil
War I was serving as assistant to a firm of
Liverpool merchants trading chiefly with India
and the United States. There was little in my
life at the outset to foretell the full taste of
danger, excitement, and adventure which it
was my fortune so early to enjoy. I had
nothing to hope for beyond the usual life of
office routine and a dim chance of a partnership
abroad in the future.

B

Young as I was, my interest in the coming
struggle was deeply aroused. From the position I occupied its significance was brought
home to me with the absorbing interest of a
factor in my career. My own fortunes and
those of my nearest friends seemed at their
outset to be bound up in a piece of history that
promised to leave its mark upon the world.
Nowhere indeed out of America was the
secession of the Southern States more keenly
watched or canvassed than in Liverpool offices
and upon the Exchange of the city, which
American trade had begotten and nursed; and
the particular aspect of the impending war
was most calculated to fill the imagination of
youngsters like myself, who were awakening
from the dreams of boyhood to the excitements
of real life.

It will be remembered that, as soon as
war was seen to be inevitable, President
Lincoln sanctioned the heroic measure of
attempting to choke secession by closing
every orifice through which supplies could be
drawn, and in the middle of April 1861
rebellion was turned into civil war by his

declaring the whole of the Southern ports in a state of blockade. One of the immediate results of this act of President Lincoln was the prompt acknowledgment of the South as belligerents by England and France. Yet the Federal States persisted in maintaining that the Confederates were rebels, and that whosoever ventured to recognise them as belligerents must be regarded as friends of rebels and no friends of the North. They ignored the fact that their interference with neutral trade, by this declaration of blockade, was a virtual concession of belligerency to the South. A declaration of blockade pre-supposes a state of war and not mere rebellion, and the claim by the Federals of a right to seize neutral vessels attempting to break a blockade was one which can be exercised only by a belligerent; exercised by any one else it is mere piracy.

The effect of the news on the Liverpool Exchange it is needless to describe. By the scratch of a foreign pen a blow that was without precedent was struck at the chief trade of the port. So prodigious indeed was this first act of war that for some time there was a doubt whether the Neutral Powers would recognise it. Only five years before the Powers assembled at Paris to wind up the Russian war had by solemn agreement declared, as the final and universal law of nations, that blockades to be binding must be effective; that is to say, that all the ports declared to be blockaded must be actually invested, or at least so closely watched by a cruising squadron that no ship can attempt to leave or enter without manifest danger of capture. Now, as the seaboard of the Seceding States extended from the river Potomac in Virginia, above Cape Hatteras, down to the Rio Grande (the southern frontier of Texas), the coast - line which the Federal Government had to watch effectively was some 3000 miles in length. It was studded, moreover, at wide intervals with ten or a dozen ports of first-rate importance.

The total fleet of the United States when the war broke out consisted of less than 150 vessels, of which fully one-third were quite unserviceable. About forty had crews;

the rest were out of commission, and of these ten or eleven of the best were lying at the Norfolk Navy Yard and fell into the hands of the Confederates. From these figures it will be seen, therefore, how impossible it was at first to maintain the blockade which the Northerners had declared, and how ineffectual it must be, seeing the length of coast-line to be watched.

With their usual energy, however, the Northerners set to work to increase their fleet; within very few weeks over 150 vessels had been purchased and equipped for sea, and more than fifty ironclads and gunboats laid down and rapidly pushed forward towards completion. In addition to these a large number of river craft were requisitioned and protected by bullet-proof iron for service on the rivers; but even with these vigorous measures the blockade was anything but effective during the first eighteen months or two years of the war. But the Northerners steadily and by almost superhuman efforts increased their fleet, and at the beginning of 1865 had so far succeeded that they possessed a fleet of nearly 700 vessels, of which some 150 were employed upon the blockade of Wilmington and Charleston alone, and patrolling their adjacent waters.

It can easily be imagined, therefore, that attempting to get in and out of those ports in the latter months of 1864 and the early ones of 1865 was a very different business from the condition of affairs which existed earlier in the war. When the above ports fell into the hands of the Northerners, the blockade, considering the nature of the coast-line and types of vessels employed as blockaders and runners, was to all intents and purposes as effective as could be expected; for the blockading fleet consisted of almost every description of craft, from the old-fashioned 60-gun frigate to the modern "Ironsides" and "Monitors," supplemented by dozens of merchant-steamers converted into gunboats— not very formidable, perhaps, as war-ships, but still dangerous to blockade-runners, especially when fast.

The Southerners, on the other hand, were practically without any navy, with the exception of a few old wooden vessels which they seized at Norfolk Navy Yard at the outbreak of the war ; and, as they were almost entirely devoid of engineering works, material, or skilled labour, they could do but little to compete with the North upon the ocean. Their naval efforts were chiefly in the direction of supplying themselves from outside sources with commerce destroyers, such as the *Alabama, Florida, Shenandoah, Georgia,* etc., though from the wretched and scanty material which they possessed they succeeded in building two or three formidable ironclads ; but their engines and armament were defective, and their crews unskilled. Notwithstanding these drawbacks, however, the *Merrimac,* one of the old wooden steamers which they had seized at Norfolk, and which they had converted into an ironclad by covering the hull with railway iron, fought a gallant fight in Hampton Roads with the celebrated *Monitor,* after having destroyed on the previous day the *Congress* and *Cumber-land,* two large Northern war-ships.

Another ironclad was also improvised by the Southerners at Mobile. She was called

the *Tennessee*, and was altogether a more formidable craft than the *Merrimac*, both as regards
armament and size, but like the *Merrimac*
was terribly defective in engine power. When
Farragut attacked Mobile she did considerable
damage to his fleet, and for a time engaged
it single-handed, but at last was forced to haul
down her flag.

The Confederates also built another small
ironclad at Wilmington on the same lines as
the *Merrimac* and *Tennessee*, but unfortunately
she ran ashore on her passage down the river,
in order to attack the blockaders outside, and
became a total wreck. In addition to the
ships I have mentioned they possessed the
Sumbter, *Rappahanock*, *Tallahassc* (steamers),
and several sailing vessels ; but with these
vessels they had no chance against their
powerful rivals in actual warfare, although the
Alabama and her consorts swept the mercantile
navy of the United States from the ocean.

Seeing how inadequate the Federal navy
was at the time when the blockade was declared,
there was certainly a strong case for treating
President Lincoln's prohibition as a mere

"paper" blockade. This, however, the British Government did not choose to do. At this time we were particularly anxious, in view of the coming International Exhibition, to stand well with all men and to be entangled in no foreign complications. Within a fortnight, therefore, of the receipt of the news, there came out a Royal Proclamation enjoining on all loyal subjects of the British Crown an attitude of strict neutrality, and solemnly admonishing them under pain of Her Majesty's displeasure to respect the Federal blockade.

Needless to say, the proclamation awakened no respect whatever for the blockade. The lecture in the latter part of it was received in the spirit in which it was issued—as a piece of mere international courtesy; and those of Her Majesty's loyal subjects who were most affected by the new situation at once took steps to make the best of it. With due respect to the pain of Her Majesty's displeasure we all knew that to run a foreign blockade could never be an offence against the laws of the realm, nor were we to be persuaded that any number of successful or

unsuccessful attempts to enter the proclaimed
ports could ever constitute a breach of neutrality. Firm after firm, with an entirely clear
conscience, set about endeavouring to recoup
itself for the loss of legitimate trade by the
high profits to be made out of successful
evasions of the Federal cruisers; and in
Liverpool was awakened a spirit the like of
which had not been known since the palmy
days of the slave trade.

It was a spirit of adventurous commerce
savouring of the good old days of the French
wars, when a lad might any day be called from
the office to take his place on the deck of a
privateer, and when daring spirits were always
ready to steal away from a convoy and run
the risk of capture on the chance of getting
the cream of the market. The risks a
blockade-runner had to face were much the
same, for as no Government pretends to
interfere with its citizens if they choose at
their peril to trade in the face of a blockade,
so no protection or redress is given them if
they are caught red-handed. After official
notification of blockade any neutral vessel

attempting to leave or enter a blockaded port forfeits its neutrality and places itself in the position of a hostile belligerent. The blockading force is entitled to treat such a ship in all respects as an enemy, and to use any means recognised in civilised warfare to drive off, capture, or destroy her. A crew so captured may be treated as prisoners of war, and their vessel carried into the captor's port, where after condemnation by an Admiralty court she becomes his prize. Nor is any resistance to capture permitted, and a single blow or shot in his own defence turns the blockade-runner into a pirate.

Such was the exciting prospect our seamen and supercargoes had before them as they sailed for the Southern ports. At first, of course, the risk was not thought very great ; the Confederate ports were so many and far between, and the Federal navy so weak and unorganised, that vessels proceeded very much as if there was no blockade at all. The consequence was that as early as June 1861, barely two months after the declaration of the blockade, several English vessels had been seized and condemned. Almost every week after that brought news of fresh captures ; on the other hand, so many ships succeeded in getting through the widely scattered cruisers, that the business still went on in the old clumsy way. We had neither of us learnt our trade then ; the Federal captains, in hopes of fat prizes, cruised without order and chased wide, leaving ports open for new-comers, while our best idea of minimising risks was to send out old unseaworthy slugs which we could well afford to lose.

During the whole of the first year of the war it was in this amateurish way that things went on. A pretty regular tale of captures came in, and among the reports the mails brought home began to be whispered stories of daring attempts, and hair-breadth escapes, that set many a youngster kicking very impatiently under his desk. There came stories, too, of exasperated or ill-conditioned Federal captains who had behaved with unwarrantable bluster or tyranny to captured crews, and these began to awaken in mercantile circles a partisan leaning towards the South, which certainly did not exist at the beginning of the war. Some of us, it must be confessed, were growing oblivious of our duty as loyal subjects and of the solemn admonitions of the proclamation of neutrality, and for not a few the profit of making a successful run began to be seasoned with the pleasure of doing a good turn to the South. It is all bygone now; runners can laugh over the rough knocks they sometimes got, and blockaders at the weary dance they were led. But in those days the ill feeling was very strong, and in the midst of all the fermenting irritation dropped the grating surprise of the *Trent* affair.

Captain Wilkes, a Federal naval officer commanding the West India station and engaged in blockade duties, took upon himself, with more zeal than law, to board the *Trent*, a British mail steamer, on the high seas, and seize from its deck two Confederate diplomatic agents who were passengers from Havana, accredited respectively to the French and the British Governments. There is no doubt that the English nation was prepared to make any sacrifice to resent this outrage, and feeling ran very deep while we waited for the answer to our demands for redress. It cannot be denied that people on the other side made themselves a little ridiculous and irritating over our perfectly reasonable request for the surrender of the prisoners. Captain Wilkes was the hero of the hour, and blustering exultation over England the tune of the street. But in the White House heads were cooler, and in due course full reparation was made. Still the "spoiled child of diplomacy" was not made to apologise — she barely expressed regret, and her omission of this international courtesy, combined with the extravagances of her press, confirmed in many Englishmen their inchoate partisanship for the South.

Such was the state of things when, one day early in the year 1862, one of the partners in the house where I was serving called me into his room. After telling me how he and a few friends had purchased a steamer to have a try at the blockade, he asked me if I would care to go as supercargo?

The answer was not doubtful. It was a stroke of luck far better than I had any right to expect at my age (for I was but twenty-one), and needless to say I embraced my fortune with alacrity.

"By all means," said I, "if I am not too young."

My chief was good enough to say that he thought I was *not* too young, and so I was fairly launched in my career as a blockade-runner.

CHAPTER II

MY FIRST ATTEMPT ON THE *DESPATCH*

The *Despatch*—A blockade-runner's cargo—The start for the West Indies—Put back to Queenstown—A terrific gale—Arrival at Nassau—The dangers of somnambulism—A haunt for buccaneers —A sleepy settlement—Neutral territory—Southern firms running the blockade—Nassau as a basis of operations—The *Despatch* condemned—Efforts to meet a more stringent blockade—"No cure no pay"—Yellow fever—Seizure of the *Despatch*—A scheme for her rescue—Her release.

WERE it only for the glimpse it gives of the state of the mercantile marine thirty years ago, my first voyage would be worth relating. Those who do not know how things were before the Plimsoll Act had made a revolution in Merchant Shipping would hardly believe what a man even in my position was expected to undergo without complaint.

The steamer that had been purchased as a blockade-runner, like most others at this time, was quite unfit for the purpose. To explain

that she was a second-hand Irish cattle boat
will convey to those who have voyaged in St.
George's Channel a fair idea of what she was.
Those who have not must understand that the
average quality and condition of such craft are
very low, and the *Despatch* was not above
the average. Her boilers were nearly worn
out; her engines had been sadly neglected;
and added to this, she drew far too much
water for the hazardous entrances of the
blockaded ports. But so indifferent were the
ships at this time composing the blockading
squadrons, so insufficient their numbers, and so
inefficient their crews, that during the first year
small sailing vessels of light draught and ordinary trading steamers were employed for the
purpose of running the blockade.

As has been shown, anything was thought
good enough for a blockade-runner then, and
no time was lost in getting a cargo on board
the *Despatch*. In choosing this there was not
much difficulty. In January a vessel flying
the Confederate colours had put into Liverpool; she had run the blockade out and was
thus able to bring us, not only the latest news

of the Federal fleet, but also full information of the kind of cargo that would be most welcome in the Southern ports.

The chief requirements were war materials of every sort, cloth for uniforms, buttons, thread, boots, stockings, and all clothing, medicines, salt, boiler-iron, steel, copper, zinc, and chemicals. As it did not pay merchants to ship heavy goods, the charge for freight per ton at Nassau being £80 to £100 in gold, a great portion of the cargo generally consisted of light goods, such as silks, laces, linens, quinine, etc., on which immense profits were made. At this time there were no mills, and practically no manufactories in the Confederate States, so their means of production were *nil.* With the progress of the war their need of war material increased so sorely that in 1864 the Confederate Government limited the freight-room on private account, and prohibited the importation of luxuries on the ground that if allowed to come in and be purchased the resources of the country would thereby be absorbed.

As soon as her lading was complete a start

was made.   And what a start it was!   It almost
takes one's breath away in these be-legislated
days to think what the *Despatch* must have
looked like as she dropped down the Mersey.
Her owners had taken advantage of their
timely information to load her down, as low
as she would float, with a cargo consisting of
ponderous cases and barrels of war material
as well as light goods; her deck was piled as
high as the rail with coal, which had to be
taken for the voyage to Nassau, so as to
avoid calling at any intermediate port; and she
steamed out to brave the Atlantic with barely
one foot of freeboard to her credit.

Fortunately at the outset the weather kept
fair, or my career must have had a very pre-
mature end; but thanks to an unusually fine
February we wallowed along pretty comfort-
ably, till we had made some 400 miles to the
south-west of Ireland.   Here, however, through
the carelessness of the engineers, the water
was allowed to get so low in the boilers that
the crowns to the furnaces of one of them were
"brought down."   This means that only by a
miracle was an explosion escaped, and that the

Despatch was entirely incapacitated from pro-
ceeding on her voyage. There was nothing to
do but to put back for repairs, under one boiler,
and we laid her head for Queenstown, thanking
our stars it was no worse.

It was three weeks before we could get to
sea again, and then it was only to find ourselves once more on the brink of destruction.
Before we had passed the Azores we came in
for a terrific gale, which our overladen vessel
was in no condition to meet; she speedily
sprang a leak, so serious that in a very short
time four of the eight furnaces were extinguished and the firemen were toiling at the
rest up to their knees in water. For hours we
looked for her to founder at any moment, as
the gray breakers came rolling upon us, but
somehow we managed to keep her afloat, and
in due course were ploughing through the
sunny waters of New Providence, and came
to rest in the pretty harbour of Nassau.

In those days I was a confirmed somnam-
bulist, and one stormy night considerably astonished the officer of the watch by suddenly
appearing on the bridge at midnight in bare

feet and sleeping attire. Gripping him by the arm I yelled, "For God's sake respect the spars," and turning on my heel returned to my cabin along the slippery deck, with the steamer pitching and rolling in half a gale of wind. Of course the man thought I was mad, but was too astonished to seize me; perhaps it was fortunate he did not do so, as to have been suddenly awakened in such a situation might have been anything but pleasant. I have for many years given up this dangerous habit. My last escapade occurred a long time ago, when one afternoon on board a P. & O. steamer, while taking a siesta, I suddenly jumped through the upper half door of my deck cabin and appeared in very light attire, to the astonished gaze of some fifty passengers who were on the quarter-deck. Fortunately a friend who was travelling with me managed to clasp me round the waist before I could jump overboard, and conducted me to my cabin none the worse, except for a skinned nose and barked shins. My fellow-passengers, however, were evidently suspicious regarding my condition of mind, and looked very much askance when I appeared at dinner, thinking no doubt that I was a lunatic and my friend my keeper.

If that voyage had been almost enough to extinguish all the ardour I had for the life before me, Nassau was enough to set it well aflame again. The very thought of the place and of the exciting life there in those days, through the brief fever of its prosperity, sets my fancy tingling even now.

Those few short years of extravagant importance—so sudden, so fitful, so completely passed away—are like a dream, and it seems almost impossible to revive a picture of what Nassau was when it found itself the base of operations against the great blockade. For centuries the little town had slumbered in complete obscurity. Depopulated and abandoned in the old days by the Spaniards, it had been occupied in Stuart times by Englishmen, and became a haunt of buccaneers. Then followed a century or so when it was a counter for diplomatists, and buccaneers settled down into wreckers, scraping together hard-earned living from the hurricanes' leavings, and filling up the dull months between the stormy seasons

with a little fruit raising and sponge fishing.
Thus ingloriously had it faded into the ob-
scurest of colonial capitals, with a population
of some 3000 or 4000 souls.   There lived and
ruled the Governor of the Bahamas, and there
lived the Chief Justice and the Bishop; these
with their modest following, and the officers
of a West India regiment and a few of the
leading merchants and their families, made up
almost all there was of society!   Little more
eventful ever broke the monotony of their
feuds and friendships than the visit of one of
the ships forming the West Indian squadron.
Their Lilliputian politics went on from year to
year, undisturbed and uncared for; there was
nothing to mark their place in the world but
a dusty pigeon-hole somewhere in the Colonial
Office, which was filled, and emptied, and filled
again.   Every one was poor and every one
lazily hopeless of any further development;
a few schooners that came and went at in-
frequent intervals sufficed for all the trade
there was, and the whole air of the sleepy
settlement had been one of indolent acqui-
escence in its own obscurity.

Then past all expectations came the war, and gold poured into its astonished lap. When first I saw the low line of houses nestling in the tropical vegetation of their gardens a change had already taken place. The blockade had been on foot a bare year, but even then the quiet little port had asserted its new importance and was overflowing with the turmoil of life. Many influential firms connected with the Southern States, and also English ones, had established agencies there, and almost every day steamers managed by those agents left the harbour to try their luck at evading the blockade or arrived with cargoes of cotton from the beleagured ports. Of course, seeing that Nassau was only some 560 miles from Charleston and 640 from Wilmington, and that, moreover, the chain of the Bahama islets extended some hundred miles in the direction of those ports, thus providing the extra protection of neutral territory for that distance, Nassau was *par excellence* the base for approaching the blockaded Atlantic ports of the South. Bermuda was its rival, but only in a lesser degree, as it was further off, and its conveniences as regards communication and accommodation were less. It is some 690 miles distant from Wilmington, the course being somewhat to the northward of west, and in the autumn especially it was seldom possible to get over without encountering a gale of wind. The one thing necessary for the blockading vessels being speed, their hulls were of the lightest description; this, coupled with the fact that they were always loaded down deep with coal, made a gale of wind an even worse enemy to encounter than a Federal cruiser.

Havana was the best base for the Gulf ports, but as New Orleans was captured early on in the war, Galveston and Mobile were the only two blockaded ports that could be approached from it; and seeing the difficulty there was in procuring cotton at those places and of disposing of inward cargoes, the trade done with them was a flea-bite compared with that from Charleston and Wilmington. At one time the trade of these two ports assumed very large proportions; the number of vessels employed in it was astonishing, and no sooner was one sunk, stranded, burnt, or captured than two more seemed to take her place.

Of Southern firms Messrs. Fraser, Trenholm, and Co. did the largest business, as they were not only engaged largely on their own account in blockade-running enterprises, but they were also agents for the Southern States Government. Their representative in Nassau, Mr. J. B. Lafitte, a charming man in every respect, occupied a most prominent position,—in fact more prominent than that of the Governor himself, and certainly he was remunerated better.

After Fraser, Trenholm, and Co. came the English firm of Alex. Collie and Co., at that time one of great repute, represented by my friend L. G. Watson, and they from time to time were possessed of a large fleet of runners commanded mostly by naval officers. After them came the house I represented, which from first to last owned some fifteen steamers; and after them a number of small firms, owning perhaps one, possibly two, boats apiece, so that in the aggregate the number of boats and the capital employed was enormous.

So nicely has Nature dispersed the Bahamas that they afforded neutral water to within fifty miles of the American coast, and no sooner was the blockade declared than the advantages of Nassau as a basis of operations were recognised and embraced. The harbour was alive with shipping, the quays were piled with cotton, the streets were thronged with busy life. So far grown and established indeed did I find the business of blockade-running, that I was seized with a sense of being late in the field and with a desire to rush in and reclaim lost time. Fortunately there was little to delay us, so, full of impatience and excitement, we set about preparing for a run. Our supplies were ready, and in the harbour lay a barque which had been sent out to act as my coal store-ship, and afterwards she was to carry home any cotton we should succeed in getting out. Nothing seemed wanting for a start, but I was doomed to disappointment. No sooner did I begin to pick up the lore of the place than the unpleasant truth came out.

Even in the early days there were men whose tales of successful trips gave them a reputation as "blockade experts," and every one of them condemned the *Despatch* as wholly unfit for the work. The blockade was already gaining system and coherence; the Northerners, no longer content with simply blockading the Confederate ports, had established a chain of powerful cruisers which patrolled the seas from the American coast to the very entrance of Nassau harbour. The old *Despatch* was much too slow to stand a ghost of a chance of escaping them, moreover she drew so much water that the Charleston bar was the only one she could hope to get over, and it was now so strictly watched that a craft so unhandy was certain to be captured in the attempt.

After all I had gone through it was a bitter pill to swallow, but it was impossible for a man entirely without experience, as I was then, to ignore the exasperating unanimity of the experts; therefore after consultation with the local agent of my firm I resolved to sell my cargoes on the spot and get both vessels home to the best advantage.

Still I was not without consolation. Although within a year of the beginning of the blockade the North, in pursuit of a steady policy, had secured various bases on the blockaded coast for the use of their squadrons, which were rapidly being augmented by improved types of vessels, and had thereby reduced considerably the number of points to be watched, and though the business of blockade-running was now becoming risky, no time was lost in endeavouring to meet the new demands on our energy and skill. If the Federals were learning the business, so were we. It was clear that the blockade-runners must not only be increased in numbers but must be improved in type. The day of sailing vessels and ordinary trading steamers was over; accordingly steamers of great speed were ordered to be built expressly for the service.

I knew that at home one of the first vessels specially built for blockade-running had been laid down and was rapidly being completed, also that she was to be placed under my charge as soon as ready. Accordingly, towards the end of the year, after making my preliminary arrangements, I went home full of hope, although sadly impatient at the year's delay caused by all the mistakes and disasters.

Before getting there, however, I had an anxious time to pass through; it was necessary to provide some employment for the *Despatch* and her consort the barque *Astoria*, and as no direct freight could be obtained for either I had to cast about for intermediate work for them. The sailing vessel I despatched to New York, and in an evil moment I made a contract, on the "no cure no pay" principle, for the *Despatch* to tow a disabled steamer to the same port, arranging to go myself in the mail steamer so as to meet both ships there.

After I had completed my Nassau business I did so, and on my arrival at New York I was disgusted to find both vessels in quarantine with yellow fever on board; also that the *Despatch* had dropped her tow off Port-Royal in a gale of wind and come on without her.

This was a pretty mess for a youngster to be in, in a strange port like New York, where everything connected with Nassau was looked upon with suspicion, and the fear of yellow fever was rampant. It was my first intimate acquaintance with the disease, but, fortunately, the cooler climate in time worked its own cure, and, after encountering innumerable quarantine difficulties, both vessels were given pratique, but not before several deaths had occurred.

In the interim the *Despatch* was seized for $30,000 at the suit of the owners of the steamer which she had attempted to tow, as damages for letting her go ; and she was only released from quarantine to find herself in the clutches of the Marshal of the port. As I had no means for providing the required security, the captain and I formed rather a mad scheme to rescue her from his clutches. The captain was to get her under weigh quietly, taking the Marshal's officer with him, while I remained behind to lull suspicion. Early one misty morning he accomplished this successfully and began to steam slowly down the Bay, but the revenue cutter lying close alongside gave the alarm, and the forts opened fire at once. For a time he held on, and was nearly out of range when the pilot, fearing, I presume, for his share in the transaction, declined to go further, and there was nothing for it but ignominiously to return. Of course all this made my position worse, but, to make a long story short, a kind friend, a prominent New York banker, went bail for me, and the *Despatch* was released and loaded for home. Finally I compromised the case for about $2000. The barque I sent on to St. John, and, following her myself by steamer, I chartered her to carry home a cargo of timber.

CHAPTER III

THE *BANSHEE* NO. 1

AFTER my disappointment it will easily be imagined how anxious I was to know how my new ship was progressing. On reaching Liverpool my first care was to visit the yard where she was being built. To my great delight I found her almost completed, and a marvel of shipbuilding as it seemed to us then. For the *Banshee*, as she was called, may claim to be a landmark not only in the development of blockade but also of marine architecture. With the exception of a boat built for Living-

D

stone of African fame, she was, I believe, the first
steel ship ever laid down.   The new blockade-
runner was a paddle boat, built of steel, on
extraordinarily fine lines, 214 feet long and 20
feet beam, and drew only 8 feet of water.   Her
masts were mere poles without yards, and with
the least possible rigging.   In order to attain
greater speed in a sea-way she was built with a
turtle-back deck forward.   She was of 217 tons
net register, and had an anticipated sea speed
of eleven knots, with a coal consumption of
thirty tons a day.   Her crew, which included
three engineers and twelve firemen, consisted
of thirty-six hands all told.

Steel ship-building was then in its infancy,
and the *Banshee* was the first of a fleet that
was soon to become famous.   There were
several similar steamers already in hand, and
although no one could tell how they would
behave when exposed to the great seas of
the Atlantic, the best results were anticipated from the strength and lightness of their
materials.   They were expected to develop
a buoyancy beyond everything that had yet
been seen, and American naval officers awaited

their arrival on the scene of activity with an interest as great as ours.

The *Banshee* was ready for sea early in 1863, and I had the satisfaction of finding myself steaming down the Mersey in the *first* steel vessel that ever crossed the Atlantic.

Like most first attempts, however, she was far from a success, and by the time we reached Queenstown she had betrayed serious defects. To begin with, the speed she developed was extremely disappointing. With the idea of protecting her boilers from shot, they had been constructed so low that they had not sufficient steam space, and, worse than this, the plates of which she was built, being only an $\frac{1}{8}$ and $\frac{3}{16}$ of an inch thick, she proved so weak that her decks leaked like a sieve. It was found absolutely necessary to put into Queenstown and make such alterations as were possible. Thus three more weeks were lost, and when at last we were able to put out again it was only to be driven back off the Fastnet by a south-westerly gale, which swept the *Banshee* clean from stem to stern of everything on deck, filled her fore stoke-hole, and compelled us to return for fresh repairs. Considering how frail the vessel was, the wonder is, not that the *Banshee* was driven back, but that she ever got across the Atlantic at all. Still her next start was successful, and reaching Madeira without adventure, excepting a close shave from being run down in the Bay of Biscay by a French barque, she began her real career as a blockade-runner.

For even here danger began. At this time a great deal of bad blood was caused by the way in which the Northerners in their efforts to enforce a blockade were extending the doctrine of the operations permissible to belligerents. But there is no doubt now that they were perfectly right. True, the proposition that a belligerent might seize a neutral ship for attempted breach of blockade thousands of miles away from the blockaded coast was one that would have been condemned by the old school of International lawyers as nothing less than monstrous, and by none more energetically than the great publicists who have so richly adorned the American bench.

So far were such doctrines from being recognised, that it was generally held that a vessel making a long ocean voyage might even call at a blockaded port to inquire if the blockade was still existent, and, no matter how suspicious her intentions, she was entitled to a warning before being captured. But it must be remembered that those were the days of sailing ships, which might have been without any news of passing events for months. No blockade of any importance had yet been subjected to the new conditions of steam navigation, and it was unreasonable to expect that the blockaders would hold themselves bound by rules which never contemplated the existing state of things. If the Americans were stretching the theory of blockade, it was only because we were extending its practice. It was not to be argued that, if we were building a whole fleet of steamers for the express purpose of defying their cruisers, they were not justified in trying to intercept them at any point they chose. From the very outset the voyages of these vessels showed them to be guilty, and the most barefaced advocate could hardly have maintained without shame that they were protected by their ostensibly neutral destination, when that destination was a notorious nest of offence like Nassau.

Still the new methods were none the less galling to the susceptibilities of British merchants, who of all men claimed to go and come on the high seas as they pleased, and every day those engaged in the service became more pronounced in their Southern sympathies, and louder in their denunciations of the Northerner's high-handed ways.

In order to economise coal the *Banshee* was taking the usual course adopted by sailing vessels. This was the ordinary practice of runners, and as the Federals grew bolder, stronger, and more exasperated, they stretched their patrolling cruisers further and further across the Atlantic, till, a few weeks after the *Banshee* left Madeira, a Federal ship of war was actually lying in wait for one of the new runners at the mouth of Funchal Bay! The moment the British vessel put to sea the American opened fire upon her as mercilessly as though she were coming out of Charleston or Wilmington instead of out of a neutral port, and nothing but superior speed and clever

handling saved her from destruction within
sight and sound of neutral territory.

The *Banshee* having been earlier in the
field was more fortunate, but the voyage was
none the less exciting as she neared the
Bahamas. The neighbouring seas were alive
with cruisers who, regarding everything
bound for Nassau as *primâ facie* guilty of an
intention to break the blockade, seized any
vessel they had a mind to on the chance of
getting her condemned in the United States
Courts. Indeed, the principal centres of
blockade-running were almost as closely
invested as the ports of the Confederate
States, and only a few months before the
notorious Captain Wilkes (now promoted to
the rank of Admiral for his popular but unwarrantable conduct in the *Trent* affair) had
been further distinguishing himself by literally
blockading Bermuda with the squadron under
his command.

Although from first to last the British
Government showed nothing but sympathy
with the Northern States in the difficult
task of their blockade, and although they

never once complained of a decision of the
American Courts, or in any way countenanced
the runners, this was going a little too far.
A protest was unavoidable, and considering the antecedents of Admiral Wilkes the
Federal Government could hardly complain
if two British war-ships were ordered to watch
the over-zealous officer. It would appear
that at the White House the representations
from St. James's were regarded as reasonable,
for after this the American cruisers kept a
more deferential distance ; the *Banshee* at any
rate was able to run into Nassau without
being overhauled, and her arrival there caused
a great sensation, as being the first boat
specially built for the service.

Having received the congratulations of my
many friends at Nassau upon possessing so
fine a tool to work with, I at once set about
getting her ready for a trip as soon as the
nights set in dark enough. For so vigilant
had the blockading force become by this time,
that a successful run was considered practically impossible except on moonless nights.
Invisibility, care, and determination were the

secrets of success, and to this end the *Banshee*
was carefully prepared.   Everything aloft was
taken down, till nothing was left standing but
the two lower masts with small cross-trees
for a look-out man on the fore, and the boats
were lowered to the level of the rails.   The
whole ship was then painted a sort of dull white,
the precise shade of which was so nicely ascertained by experience before the end of the
war that a properly dressed runner on a dark
night was absolutely indiscernible at a cable's
length.   So particular were captains on this
point that some of them even insisted on their
crews wearing white at night, holding that
one black figure on the bridge or on deck was
enough to betray an otherwise invisible vessel.

Perfect as the *Banshee* looked, when her
toilet was complete, I was even more fortunate
in my crew.

For captain I had Steele, one of the
most daring and successful commanders the
time brought out.   Absolutely devoid of fear,
never flurried, decided and ready in emergency, and careful as a mother, he was the
beau-ideal of a blockade-runner.   Already he

had served his apprenticeship to the trade
and knew what failure meant, for while in
command of the *Tubal Cain* he had been
captured on his very first trip, and, after
tasting for a short time the hospitality of an
American prison, had been released—richer by
the experience, but in no wise daunted.

The chief engineer, Erskine, too, had seen
service, having worked as second engineer on
board the Confederate cruiser *Oreto*, when the
famous Captain Maffitt ran her into Savannah.
As the engines of a blockade-runner are her
arm, her success must necessarily in great
measure depend on the qualities of her
engineer, and it would have been hard to find
a better man for the task than Erskine. Cool
in danger, full of resource in sudden difficulty,
and as steady as the tide, he was yet capable
of fearlessly risking everything and straining
to the last pound, when the word came, in one
of those rousing forms of expression with
which old Steele was wont to notify down the
engine-room tube, that the critical moment
had come.

For pilot a Wilmington man had been

sent out by our agents there, and was waiting for me at Nassau. He too turned out a jewel. He knew his port like his own face, and the most trying situations or heaviest firing could never put him off or disturb his serene self-possession. For all his duties he had an instinct that approached genius. On the blackest night he could always make out a blockader several minutes before any one else; and so acute at last did this sense become, that it used to be a byword that Tom Burroughs at last got to smell a cruiser long before he could see her.

Through the ignorance or cowardice of the pilot vessels were frequently lost, and to obtain a good pilot was as troublesome as it was essential. The risk they ran was great, for if captured they were never exchanged; but their pay, which frequently amounted to £700 or £800 a round trip, was proportionate to the risk.

Thus well equipped and laden with arms, gunpowder, boots, and all kinds of contraband of war, as soon as the moon was right, the *Banshee* stole out of Nassau for the first time to make the best of her way to Wilmington.

CHAPTER IV

WILMINGTON was the first port I attempted; in fact with the exception of one run to Galveston it was always our destination. It had many advantages. Though furthest from Nassau it was nearest to headquarters at Richmond, and from its situation was very difficult to watch effectively. It was here, moreover, that my firm had established its agency as soon as they had resolved to take up the blockade-running business. The town itself lies some sixteen miles up the Cape Fear river, which falls into the ocean at a point

where the coast forms the sharp salient angle
from which the river takes its name. Off its
mouth lies a delta, known as Smith's Island,

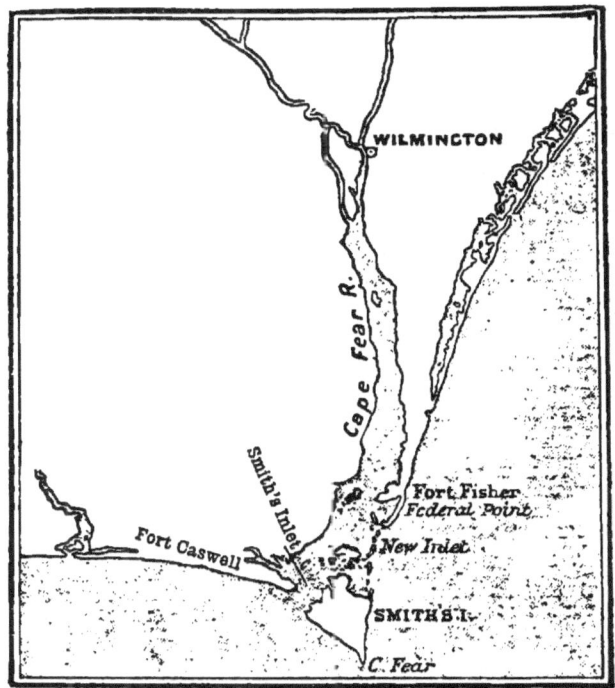

PLAN OF WILMINGTON HARBOUR.

which not only emphasises the obnoxious
formation of the coast, but also divides the
approach to the port into two widely separated
channels, so that in order to guard the approach

to it a blockading force is compelled to divide into two squadrons.

At one entrance of the river lies Fort Fisher, a work so powerful that the blockaders instead of lying in the estuary were obliged to form roughly a semicircle out of range of its guns, and the falling away of the coast on either side of the entrance further increased the extent of ground they had to cover. The system they adopted in order to meet the difficulty was extremely well conceived, and, did we not know to the contrary, it would have appeared complete enough to ensure the capture of every vessel so foolhardy as to attempt to enter or come out.

Across either entrance an inshore squadron was stationed at close intervals. In the daytime the steamers composing this squadron anchored, but at night they got under weigh and patrolled in touch with the flagship, which, as a rule, remained at anchor. Further out there was a cordon of cruisers, and outside these again detached gun-boats keeping at such a distance from the coast as they calculated a runner coming out would traverse between the time of high water on Wilmington bar and sunrise, so that if any blockade-runner coming out got through the two inner lines in the dark she had every chance of being snapped up at daybreak by one of the third division.

Besides these special precautions for Wilmington there must not be forgotten the ships engaged in the general service of the blockade, consisting, in addition to those detailed to watch Nassau and other bases, of free cruisers that patrolled the Gulf-stream. From this it will be seen readily, that from the moment the *Banshee* left Nassau harbour till she had passed the protecting forts at the mouth of Cape Fear river, she and those on board her could never be safe from danger or free for a single hour from anxiety. But, although at this time the system was already fairly well developed, the Northerners had not yet enough ships at work to make it as effective as it afterwards became.

The *Banshee's* engines proved so unsatisfactory that under ordinary conditions nine or ten knots was all we could get out of her; she was therefore not permitted to run any avoidable risks, and to this I attribute her extraordinary success where better boats failed. As long as daylight lasted a man was never out of the cross-trees, and the moment a sail was seen the *Banshee's* stern was turned to it till it was dropped below the horizon. The look-out man, to quicken his eyes, had a dollar for every sail he sighted, and if it were seen from the deck first he was fined five. This may appear excessive, but the importance in blockade-running of seeing before you are seen is too great for any chance to be neglected; and it must be remembered that the pay of ordinary seamen for each round trip in and out was from £50 to £60.

Following these tactics we crept noiselessly along the shores of the Bahamas, invisible in the darkness, and ran on unmolested for the first two days out, though our course was often interfered with by the necessity of avoiding hostile vessels ; then came the anxious moment on the third, when, her position having been taken at noon to see if she was near enough to run under the guns of Fort Fisher before the following daybreak, it was found there was just time, but none to spare for accidents or delay.

Still the danger of lying out another day so close to the blockaded port was very great, and rather than risk it we resolved to keep straight on our course and chance being overtaken by daylight before we were under the Fort.

Now the real excitement began, and nothing I have ever experienced can compare with it. Hunting, pig-sticking, steeple-chasing, big-game shooting, polo—I have done a little of each—all have their thrilling moments, but none can approach " running a blockade " ; and perhaps my readers can sympathise with my enthusiasm when they consider the dangers to be encountered, after three days of constant anxiety and little sleep, in threading our way through a swarm of blockaders, and the accuracy required to hit in the nick of time the mouth of a river only half a mile wide, without lights and with a coast-line so low and featureless that as a rule the first intimation we had of its nearness was the dim white line of the surf.

There were of course many different plans of getting in, but at this time the favourite dodge was to run up some fifteen or twenty miles to the north of Cape Fear, so as to round

E

the northernmost of the blockaders, instead of
dashing right through the inner squadron ;
then to creep down close to the surf till the
river was reached : and this was the course the
Banshee intended to adopt.

We steamed cautiously on until nightfall :
the night proved dark, but dangerously clear
and calm. No lights were allowed—not even
a cigar ; the engine-room hatchways were
covered with tarpaulins, at the risk of suffocat-
ing the unfortunate engineers and stokers in
the almost insufferable atmosphere below. But
it was absolutely imperative that not a glimmer
of light should appear. Even the binnacle
was covered, and the steersman had to see
as much of the compass as he could through
a conical aperture carried almost up to his eyes.

With everything thus in readiness we
steamed on in silence except for the stroke
of the engines and the beat of the paddle-floats,
which in the calm of the night seemed distress-
ingly loud ; all hands were on deck, crouching
behind the bulwarks ; and we on the bridge,
namely, the captain, the pilot, and I, were
straining our eyes into the darkness. Pre-

sently Burroughs made an uneasy movement—
" Better get a cast of the lead, Captain," I
heard him whisper. A muttered order down
the engine-room tube was Steele's reply, and
the *Banshee* slowed and then stopped. It was
an anxious moment, while a dim figure stole
into the fore-chains ; for there is always a
danger of steam blowing off when engines are
unexpectedly stopped, and that would have
been enough to betray our presence for miles
around. In a minute or two came back the
report, "sixteen fathoms—sandy bottom with
black specks." "We are not as far in as I
thought, Captain," said Burroughs, "and we
are too far to the southward. Port two points
and go a little faster." As he explained, we
must be well to the northward of the speckled
bottom before it was safe to head for the shore,
and away we went again. In about an hour
Burroughs quietly asked for another sounding.
Again she was gently stopped, and this time
he was satisfied. "Starboard and go ahead
easy," was the order now, and as we crept in
not a sound was heard but that of the regular beat of the paddle-floats still dangerously

loud in spite of our snail's pace. Suddenly
Burroughs gripped my arm,—

"There's one of them, Mr. Taylor," he
whispered, "on the starboard bow."

In vain I strained my eyes to where he
pointed, not a thing could I see; but presently
I heard Steele say beneath his breath, "All
right, Burroughs, I see her. Starboard a little,
steady!" was the order passed aft.

A moment afterwards I could make out a long
low black object on our starboard side, lying
perfectly still. Would she see us? that was
the question; but no, though we passed within
a hundred yards of her we were not discovered,
and I breathed again. Not very long after
we had dropped her Burroughs whispered,—

"Steamer on the port bow."

And another cruiser was made out close
to us.

"Hard-a-port," said Steele, and round she
swung, bringing our friend upon our beam.
Still unobserved we crept quietly on, when all
at once a third cruiser shaped herself out of
the gloom right ahead and steaming slowly
across our bows.

"Stop her," said Steele in a moment, and as we lay like dead our enemy went on and disappeared in the darkness. It was clear there was a false reckoning somewhere, and that instead of rounding the head of the blockading line we were passing through the very centre of it. However, Burroughs was now of opinion that we must be inside the squadron and advocated making the land. So "slow ahead" we went again, until the low-lying coast and the surf line became dimly visible. Still we could not tell where we were, and, as time was getting on alarmingly near dawn, the only thing to do was to creep down along the surf as close in and as fast as we dared. It was a great relief when we suddenly heard Burroughs say, "It's all right, I see the 'Big Hill'!"

The "Big Hill" was a hillock about as high as a full-grown oak tree, but it was the most prominent feature for miles on that dreary coast, and served to tell us exactly how far we were from Fort Fisher. And fortunate it was for us we were so near. Daylight was already breaking, and before we were opposite the fort we could make out six or seven gunboats, which steamed rapidly towards us and angrily opened fire. Their shots were soon dropping close around us : an unpleasant sensation when you know you have several tons of gunpowder under your feet. To make matters worse, the North Breaker shoal now compelled us to haul off the shore and steam further out. It began to look ugly for us, when all at once there was a flash from the shore followed by a sound that came like music to our ears—that of a shell whirring over our heads. It was Fort Fisher, wide awake and warning the gunboats to keep their distance. With a parting broadside they steamed sulkily out of range, and in half an hour we were safely over the bar. A boat put off from the fort and then,—well, it was the days of champagne cocktails, riot whiskies and sodas—and one did not run a blockade every day. For my part, I was mightily proud of my first attempt and my baptism of fire. Blockade-running seemed the pleasantest and most exhilarating of pastimes. I did not know then what a very serious business it could be.

CHAPTER V

IT was now that I made the acquaintance—
soon to ripen into a warm friendship—of
Colonel William Lamb, the Commandant of
Fort Fisher,—a man of whose courtesy,
courage, and capacity all the English who
knew him spoke in the highest terms. Origin-
ally a Virginian lawyer and afterwards the
editor of a newspaper, he volunteered at the
outbreak of the war, and rising rapidly to the
grade of colonel was given the command of
Fort Fisher, a post which he filled with high

distinction till its fall in 1865. With the
blockade-runners he was immensely popular ;
always on the alert and ever ready to reach a
helping hand, he seemed to think no exertion
too great to assist their operations, and many
a smart vessel did his skill and activity snatch
from the very jaws of the blockaders. He
came to be regarded by the runners as their
guardian angel ; and it was no small support
in the last trying moments of a run to
remember who was in Fort Fisher.

So much did we value his services and so
grateful were we for them, that at my suggestion
my firm subsequently presented him with a
battery of six Whitworth guns, of which he was
very proud ; and good use he made of them in
keeping the blockaders at a respectful distance.
They were guns with a great range, which
many a cruiser found to its cost when ventur-
ing too close in chase down the coast. Lamb
would gallop them down behind the sandhills,
by aid of mules, and open fire upon the enemy
before he was aware of his danger. Neither
must I forget his charming wife (alas, now
numbered among the majority) ; her hospitality

PORTRAIT OF COLONEL LAMB. *To face page* 36.

and kindness were unbounded, and many a pleasant social evening have I and my brother blockade-runners spent in her little cottage outside the fort.

The following extract from *Southern Historical Papers*, written by Colonel Lamb a few years ago, will doubtless interest my readers; also the account, copied from the *Wilmington Messenger*, of a meeting which took place lately between him and General Curtis at Fort Fisher.

In the fall of 1857 a lovely Puritan maiden, still in her teens, was married in Grace Church, Providence, Rhode Island, to a Virginia youth, just passed his majority, who brought her to his home in Norfolk, a typical ancestral homestead, where beside the "white folks" there was quite a colony of family servants, from the pickaninny just able to crawl to the old gray-headed mammy who had nursed "ole massa." She soon became enamoured of her surroundings and charmed with the devotion of her coloured maid, whose sole duty it was to wait upon her young missis. When the John Brown raid burst upon the South and her husband was ordered to Harper's Ferry, there was not a more indignant matron in all Virginia, and when at last secession came, the South did not contain a more enthusiastic little rebel.

On the 15th of May 1862, a few days after the surrender of Norfolk to the Federals, by her father-in-law, then mayor, amid the excitement attending a captured city, her son Willie was born. Cut off from her husband and subjected to the privations and annoyances incident to a subjugated community, her father insisted upon her coming with her children to his home in Providence ; but, notwithstanding she was in a luxurious home, with all that paternal love could do for her, she preferred to leave all these comforts to share with her husband the dangers and privations of the South.   She vainly tried to persuade Stanton, Secretary of War, to let her and her three children, with a nurse, return to the South ; finally he consented to let her go by flag of truce from Washington to City Point, but without a nurse, and as she was unable to manage three little ones, she left the youngest with his grandparents, and with two others bravely set out for Dixie.   The generous outfit of every description which was prepared for the journey, and which was carried to the place of embarkation, was ruthlessly cast aside by the inspectors on the wharf, and no tears or entreaties or offers of reward by the parents availed to pass anything save a scanty supply of clothing and other necessaries.   Arriving in the South, the brave young mother refused the proffer of a beautiful home in Wilmington, the occupancy of the grand old mansion at " Orton," on the Cape Fear river, but insisted upon taking up her abode with her children and their coloured nurse in the upper room of a pilot's house, where they lived until the soldiers of the garrison built her a cottage one mile north of Fort Fisher, on the Atlantic beach.   In both of these homes she was occasionally exposed to the shot and shell fired from blockaders at belated blockade-runners.

It was a quaint abode, constructed in most primitive style, with three rooms around one big chimney, in which North Carolina pine knots supplied heat and light on winter nights.   This cottage became historic, and was famed for the frugal but tempting meals which its charming hostess would prepare for her distinguished guests.   Besides the many illustrious Confederate Army and Navy officers who were delighted to find this bit of sunshiny civilisation on the wild sandy beach, ensconced among the sand dunes and straggling pines and black-jack, many celebrated English naval officers enjoyed its hospitality under assumed names :—Roberts, afterwards the renowned Hobart Pasha, who commanded the Turkish navy ; Murray, now Admiral Murray-Aynsley, long since retired, after having been rapidly promoted for gallantry and meritorious services in the British navy ; the brave but unfortunate Hugh Burgoyne, V.C., who went down in the British iron-clad, *Captain*, in the Bay of Biscay ; and the chivalrous Hewett, who won the Victoria Cross in the Crimea and was knighted for his services as ambassador to King John of Abyssinia, and who, after commanding the Queen's yacht, died lamented as Admiral Hewett.   Besides these there were many genial and gallant merchant captains, among them Halpin, who afterwards commanded the *Great Eastern* while laying ocean cables ; and famous war correspondents—Hon. Francis C. Lawley, M.P., correspondent of the *London Times*, and Frank Vizitelli of the *London Illustrated News*, afterwards murdered in the Soudan.   Nor must the plucky Tom Taylor be forgotten, supercargo of the *Banshee* and the *Night Hawk*, who, by his coolness and daring, escaped with a boat's crew from the hands of the Federals after capture off the fort, and who was endeared to the children as the " Santa Claus " of the war.

At first the little Confederate was satisfied with pork and potatoes, corn-bread and rye coffee, with sorghum sweetening ; but after the blockade-runners made her acquaintance the impoverished store-room was soon filled to overflowing, notwithstanding her heavy requisitions on it for the post hospital, the sick and wounded soldiers and sailors always being a subject of her tenderest solicitude, and often the hard worked and poorly fed coloured hands blessed the little lady of the cottage for a tempting treat.

Full of stirring events were the two years passed in the cottage on Confederate Point. The drowning of Mrs. Rose Greenough, the famous Confederate spy, off Fort Fisher, and the finding of her body, which was tenderly cared for, and the rescue from the waves, half dead, of Professor Holcombe, and his restoration, were incidents never to be forgotten. Her fox-hunting with horse and hounds, the narrow escapes of friendly vessels, the fights over blockade-runners driven ashore, the execution of deserters, and the loss of an infant son, whose little spirit went out with the tide one sad summer night, all contributed to the reality of this romantic life.

When Porter's fleet appeared off Fort Fisher, December 1864, it was storm-bound for several days, and the little family with their household goods were sent across the river to "Orton," before Butler's powder-ship blew up. After the Christmas victory over Porter and Butler, the little heroine insisted upon coming back to her cottage, although her husband had procured a home of refuge in Cumberland county. General Whiting protested against her running the risk, for on dark nights her husband could not leave the fort, but she said, "if the firing became too hot she would run behind the sand hills as she had done before," and come she would.

The fleet reappeared unexpectedly on the night of the 12th of January 1865. It was a dark night, and when the lights of the fleet were reported her husband sent a courier to the cottage to instruct her to pack up quickly and be prepared to leave with children and nurse as soon as he could come to bid them good-bye. The garrison barge, with a trusted crew, was stationed at Craig's Landing, near the cottage. After midnight, when all necessary orders were given for the coming attack, the colonel mounted his horse and rode to the cottage, but all was dark and silent. He found the message had been delivered,

but his brave wife had been so undisturbed by the news,
that she had fallen asleep and no preparations for a retreat
had been made.   Precious hours had been lost, and as
the fleet would soon be shelling the beach and her husband
have to return to the fort, he hurried them into the boat as
soon as dressed, with only what could be gathered up
hastily, leaving dresses, toys, and household articles to fall
into the hands of the foe.

The extraordinary circumstance occurred yesterday of
a visit to Fort Fisher by General N. M. Curtis and Colonel
William Lamb, who were pitted against each other in deadly
strife at that historic spot on the occurrence of both the
battles there during the civil war—the one commencing
24th December 1864 and the other 13th January 1865.

Colonel Lamb was in Washington a few days ago, and
made an engagement with General Curtis to visit the old
fort.   They consequently met in Norfolk last Thursday
morning and came on to Wilmington, arriving here that
night.   Yesterday morning they took the steamer *Wilmington*
at 9.30 o'clock and, accompanied by T. W. Clawson of the
Messenger, the three were landed at the Rocks and were
sent ashore in one of the *Wilmington's* small boats, the
gangway and wharf having been swept away during the gale
of 13th October.

From the Rocks the party walked to Fort Fisher, and
together the old heroes went from one end of the fort to
the other, identifying Colonel Lamb's headquarters and
locating the position of the batteries, the magazines, the
salients, the sally-port, and other historic spots.

General Curtis explained the route of his advance upon
the fort at the last battle, when the fort was captured, and
pointed out the portion of the parapet which he assaulted
and scaled, and where the first flag of the invading army
was planted on the ramparts.   The batteries at which the

first fierce hand-to-hand fights occurred were discussed as
the party walked over them, and General Curtis pointed out
about the spot inside the works where he fell, desperately and
almost fatally wounded by a piece of shell that struck him
over the left eye, and carried away a large piece of the frontal
bone and destroyed the eye.   He was believed to be killed,
and when some of his soldiers were ordered to take him to the
rear, so that his body could be shipped North, they dragged
his body over the rough ground for some distance, so that
his clothing was torn and his back was bleeding from cuts
made by such rough treatment.   Orders had been given for
a box in which to ship his body to his home in New York.

Colonel Lamb, the hero on the Confederate side, who
was in command of the fort at both battles, explained the
positions held by the brave defenders of the fort, and also
pointed out about the spot where he was shot down, a
Minie ball having broken his hip, and also where General
Whiting received his death wound.   Strange to say, all
three were wounded within a few yards of each other.
Colonel Lamb's wound came within an ace of proving fatal,
and, as it was, he was on crutches for several years.

The old fort is now a heap of ruins, consisting of
mounds of sand, where the batteries were stationed.   In
front of the land face from which the assault was made
by the United States' troops under General Curtis, and
right on the position held by his regiment, the recent storm
has unearthed a great many bones of the brave fellows
who fell in the battle.   It is not known whether they wore
the blue or the gray, but it is quite probable that they were
some of General Curtis's troops.

From the fort the party proceeded up the beach for a
mile and a half, and visited the cottage which Colonel Lamb
occupied with his family and made his general headquarters.
It is now occupied by a fisherman.   From Craig's Landing
near by the party took a sail boat and were carried back to

the Rocks by the Craig brothers. When the boat was run
ashore it grounded in shallow water about fifteen feet from
dry land, and the only alternative left was to strip shoes
and foot-wear, and roll up pants and wade out. General
Curtis, who is a man of powerful frame and sound health,
soon stepped over the boat's side and into the water,
and as Colonel Lamb's health made him cautious about
going into the water, General Curtis offered to carry him
on his back to dry land. The *Messenger* representative
being a duffer of good frame and strength, and being the
younger by half, interposed in relief of General Curtis, and
so Colonel Lamb rode the scribe to the shore. The newspaper man then wanted to kick himself for not allowing
Colonel Lamb to ride his "friend the enemy," for he could
have witnessed the remarkable instance of a brave and
distinguished Federal officer carrying on his back the
illustrious Confederate who, in years that are gone, was
raising old Harry with shot and shell to keep the General
at a safe distance. These two men were heroes of the
right stripe, and we can raise our hats in honour and
admiration of them for the rich heritage which their
manhood and bravery leaves to Americans.

After accepting the hospitality of Mr. Henry Wood, a
fisherman at the Rocks, who had prepared some coffee and
oysters for the party, the *Wilmington* came in sight at
3 o'clock, and she was boarded for the return to Wilmington.
On the trip down Colonel Lamb had bought a lot of fine
fat coots to be cooked for lunch at the Rocks, but he
forgot these, and they were left on the steamer. Imagine
the happiness of the party when they got aboard to find
that the courteous Captain John Harper had had the birds
cooked and sent them in with some delightful bread.

General Curtis and Colonel Lamb, after returning to the
city, were hospitably entertained at the Cape Fear Club.

General Curtis was a Colonel at the assault on Fort

Fisher, but he won his General's epaulettes there. By the
way, he was wounded in six places on the day the fort
was captured. He served four years and eight months in
the Federal army, having volunteered in April 1861.—
Wilmington (N. C.) *Messenger.*

After this digression I must return to our
movements on board the *Banshee.* Having
obtained pratique (for the quarantine was very
strict) and a local pilot, rendered necessary
by the river being unbuoyed and strewn with
torpedoes, we ran up at once to Wilmington.
Here I found our agent Tom Power, who had
an outward cargo ready for me, and the cheer-
ful heartiness with which the slaves set about
discharging our inward one was a pleasant
surprise; if I hadn't been told they *were* slaves
I should never have discovered it. Everything
had to be done at high pressure, for it was
important to get out as quickly as possible, so as
to try another run while the dark nights lasted,
and loading went merrily on. I therefore did
my best to win the goodwill of the officials,
on whose favour I was of course in a great
measure dependent for a rapid turn round.

Wilmington was already sadly pinched and
war-worn. There never was too much to eat

and drink there, and the commonest luxuries
were almost things of the past; so when it
became known that there was practically open
house on board the *Banshee* friends flocked to
her. She soon attained great popularity, and
it was really a sight when our luncheon bell
rang to see guests, invited and uninvited, turn
up from all quarters. We made them all
welcome, and when our little cabin was filled
we generally had an overflow meeting on deck.

What a pleasure it was to see them eat
and drink! Men who had been accustomed to
live on corn-bread and bacon, and to drink
nothing but water, appreciated our delicacies;
our bottled beer, good brandy, and, on great
occasions, our champagne, warmed their hearts
towards us. The chief steward used to look
at me appealingly, as a hint that our stores
would never last out; in fact we were often
on very short commons before we got back
to Nassau. But we had our reward. If any
special favour were asked it was always
granted, if possible, to the *Banshee*, and if any
push had to be made there was always some
one to make it.

F

Whether due to the luncheon parties or not need not be said, but we were within a very few days able to cast off our moorings and drop down the river ballasted with tobacco and laden with cotton—three tiers even on deck. Such things are almost incredible nowadays. The reckless loading, to which high profits and the perquisites allowed to officers led, is to a landsman inconceivable. That men should be found willing to put to sea at all in these frail craft piled like hay waggons is extraordinary enough, but that they should do so in the face of a vigilant and active blockading force, and do it successfully, seems rather an invention of romance than a commonplace occurrence of our own time. True, running out was a much easier matter than running in, for the risks inseparable from making a port, so difficult to find as Wilmington, without lights, and with constant change of courses, were absent, and as soon as the bar was crossed navigation at least gave no anxiety.

Steele and I had hit on a plan for getting out that promised almost a certainty of success. Its security lay in its impudence, a cardinal

virtue of blockade-running, which, as will be
seen later on in some of the more critical
scenes, approached the sublime.   The idea was
perhaps obvious enough.   As has been said,
the flagship during the night remained at
anchor, while the other ships moved slowly to
and fro upon the inner line, leaving, as was
natural enough, a small area round the Admiral's
ship unpatrolled.   This was enough for us.
Bringing up the *Banshee* behind Fort Fisher,
where she could lie hidden from the blockaders
till nightfall, we rowed ashore to get from
Colonel Lamb the last news of the squadron's
movements and to ascertain which ship bore
the Admiral's flag.   She proved to be the
Minnesota, a large sixty-gun frigate : her
bearings were accurately taken, and as soon as
night fell the *Banshee* stole quietly from her
concealment, slipped over the bar, dark as it
was, and by the aid of Steele's observations
ran in perfect security close by the flagship and
out to sea well clear of the first cordon.

In trying to pass the second, however, we
were less successful, for we ran right across a
gunboat ; she saw us and at once opened fire ;

but slow as the *Banshee* was, luckily the Northern gunboats for the most part were slower still, so we had no difficulty in increasing the distance between us till it was felt we were out of sight again. Our helm was then put hard over, giving us a course at right angles to the one we had been steaming, and after keeping it a few minutes we stopped. It was a manœuvre nearly always successful, provided the helm was not put over too soon, and this time it achieved the usual result. As we lay perfectly still, watching the course of the gunboat by the flashes of her guns and by the rockets she was sending up to attract her consorts, we had the satisfaction of seeing her labouring furiously past us and firing wildly into black space.

There still remained the danger at daybreak of the third cordon, and with anxious eyes the horizon was scoured as the darkness began to fail. A daylight chase with the *Banshee* in her present condition could not be thought of, but fortunately not a sign of a cruiser was to be seen. All that day, and the next and the next, we steamed onward with our hearts in our mouths, turning our stern to every sail or

patch of smoke that was seen, till, on the evening of the third day, we steamed into Nassau as
proudly as a heavy list to starboard would
allow.

So ended my first attempt, a triumphant
success! Besides the inward freight of £50 a
ton on the war material, I had earned by the
tobacco ballast alone £7000, the freight for
which had been paid at the rate of £70 a ton.
But this was a flea-bite compared to the profit
on the 500 odd bales of cotton we had on
board, which was at least £50 per bale.

No wonder I took kindly to my new calling,
and no wonder I at once set to work to get the
Banshee reloaded for another run before the
moonless nights were over.

CHAPTER VI

THE REST OF THE *BANSHEE* NO. I.'S CAREER

To give in detail every trip of the *Banshee* would be wearisome. I made in her seven more in all, each one of which had its peculiar excitement. Looking back it seems nothing short of a miracle that, ill-constructed and ill-engined as she was, she so long escaped the numerous dangers to which she was exposed. I well remember, on our second run in, an accident which no one could have foreseen, and which came within an ace of ending her career.

After a busy time discharging our cargo and getting coaled and loaded in order to save a trip before the moon grew too much, we made another start, and after a rough passage reached within striking distance of our port. It was a very dark but calm night; we had made out several blockaders and safely eluded them, when suddenly a tearing and rending of wood was heard, and splinters from our port paddle-box fell in all directions. The engines were stopped at once; it was then discovered that one of the paddle-floats, which were made of steel, had split, causing the broken part to come violently in contact with the paddle-box at each revolution. There was nothing for it but to stop and attempt to unscrew the damaged float; a sail was placed round the paddle-box and two of the engineers were lowered down and commenced work: not many minutes elapsed before a cruiser hove in sight, and we made certain we had been discovered. Although she came on until she was not more than a hundred yards away on our beam, curious to state she never saw us, but, after lying motionless, much to our relief she steamed away, and oh! how pleasant it was to hear that float drop into the water.

We felt our way towards the bar, and although we were heavily peppered by two gunboats which were lying close in, we escaped untouched and soon had our signal lights set for going over the bar. These signal lights were of course a great assistance, but latterly the Northerners used to place launches close in, and when those in charge saw the lights exhibited they signalled to the blockaders, who immediately commenced shelling the bar, rendering it very unpleasant for us ; so much so that we generally preferred to find our way over it without lights, as the lesser risk of the two. It was the custom for each steamer to carry a Confederate signalman, who by means of a code could communicate with the shore, in the daytime with flags, at night by flashes from lamps. If the leading lights were required, the pilots in the fort set two lights which, when in line, led us through deep water over the bar.

This was an average run in, but more exciting ones were to follow. In the earlier stages of blockade-running, such as those I have mentioned, we used to go well to the northward and make the coast some fifteen or twenty miles above Fort Fisher, thus going round the fleet instead of through it. By this means we were the better enabled to strike the coast unobserved, steaming quietly down, just outside the surf, until we arrived close to Fort Fisher, where we had to go somewhat to seaward, in order to avoid a certain shoal called the North Breaker. Although this generally brought us into close contact with the blockaders, still we knew exactly where we were as regards the bar. Subsequently the Northerners stopped this manoeuvre, as we found to our peril.

One very dark night (I think it was either on the fourth or fifth trip of the *Banshee*) we made the land about twelve miles above Fort Fisher, and were creeping quietly down as usual, when all at once we made a cruiser out, lying on our port-bow, and slowly moving about two hundred yards from the shore. It

was a question of going inside or outside her ;
if we went outside she was certain to see us,
and would chase us into the very jaws of the
fleet. As we had very little steam up we
chose the former alternative, hoping to pass
unobserved between the cruiser and the shore,
aided by the dark background of the latter.
It was an exciting moment ; we got almost
abreast of her, as we thought, unobserved,
and success seemed within our grasp, till
we saw her move in towards us and heard her
hail us as we came on, "Stop that steamer or
I will sink you"!

Old Steele growled out that we hadn't time
to stop, and shouted down the engine-room
tube to Erskine to pile on the coals, as
concealment was no longer of any use. Our
friend, which we afterwards found out was
the *Niphon*, opened fire as fast as she could
and sheered close into us, so close that her
boarders were called away twice, and a
slanging match went on between us, like that
sometimes to be heard between two penny
steamboat captains on the Thames. She
closed the dispute by shooting away our fore

mast, exploding a shell in our bunkers, and, when we began to leave her astern, by treating us to grape and canister. It was a miracle that no one was killed, but the crew were all lying flat on the deck, except the steersman; and at one time I fear he did the same, for as Pilot Burroughs suddenly cried, "My God, Mr. Taylor, look there"! I saw our boat heading right into the surf, so, jumping from the bridge, I ran aft and found the helmsman on his stomach. I rushed at the wheel and got two or three spokes out of it, which hauled her head off the land, but it was a close shave.

Two miles farther on we picked up another cruiser, which tried to treat us in a similar manner, but as we had plenty of steam we soon left her. A little farther we came across a large side-wheel boat, which tried to run us down, missing us only by a few yards; after that we were unmolested and arrived in safe, warmly congratulated by Lamb, who thought from the violent cannonade that we must certainly have been sunk.

Not more than one man out of a hundred

would have brought a boat through as Steele
did that night,—the other ninety-nine would
have run her ashore.

After this exciting run-in our first business
was to repair damages and ship our cargo on
board; but at the last moment, when she was
completely loaded, with steam up and all ready
for a start, we nearly lost the *Banshee* by fire.
Steele and I were busy settling things in the
office on shore, when all at once, on looking
out of the window, I saw volumes of smoke
coming from her deck cargo of cotton; we
jumped into a boat, but by the time we got
alongside she was one sheet of flame. It
looked like a hopeless case. Steele, however,
gave immediate orders to get the steam hose
at work, breast her off from the wharf, and to
let go anchor in mid stream; thus bringing
her head to tide, but stern to wind. The fire,
being all forward, made it difficult to reach
the forecastle so as to let go the anchor; but
our good friend Halpin (who then commanded
a blockade-runner called the *Eugénie*) gallantly
came to our assistance, at the risk of his life
boarded us forward, and knocked out the

cutter which held the chain cable, but not before his clothes were on fire : it was a sight to see him take a header into the river, causing the water to hiss again. He undoubtedly saved our ship that day. Poor Halpin—I have lately read of his death—he was as fine and generous-hearted a man as ever lived, and was afterwards as successful at cable-laying as blockade-running.

By dint of hard work we got the fire under, and a tough job it was fighting with ignited turpentine, of which we had several barrels on deck, and blazing cotton. We found that, with the exception of having our turtle back destroyed and our deck, bulwarks, and new foremast charred, she had not received much serious damage, and after shipping a fresh deck cargo we went to sea next night and crossed to Nassau, where they were astonished to see the plight we were in, thinking we had had a fire at sea.

It was, I think, on our sixth trip out in the little *Banshee*, when soon after daylight we had got safely through the fleet, and I was lying on a cotton bale aft, that Erskine, the chief engineer, suddenly exclaimed, " Mr. Taylor, look astern "!

I looked, and not four miles from us I saw
a large side-wheel cruiser, with square sails
set, coming down on us hand over fist. This
was an instance of gross carelessness on the
part of the look-out man at the masthead
(he turned out to be an American whom we
had shipped in Nassau, on the previous trip,
and about whom both Steele and I had our private suspicions). At such a critical moment as
the approach of daylight the chief officer should
have chosen a picked man for the look-out.
After this we were more careful : either the
chief officer or I myself, when on board, making
it a point to occupy this post at that particular hour.

Erskine rushed to the engine-room, and in a
few moments volumes of smoke issuing from
our funnels showed that we were getting up all
the steam we could—almost too late, as with the
freshening breeze the chaser (which we afterwards found out to be the well-known *James
Adger*, a boat subsequently sent to cruise in
search of the *Alabama*) so rapidly overhauled us
that we could distinctly see the officers in uniform
as they stood on the bridge ; each one, doubtless,

THE RAMBLER CHASED BY TWO SHARK.

To face page 73.

counting his share of the prize money to which he would soon become entitled.

"This will never do," said Steele, who, although it put us off our course to Nassau, ordered the helm to be altered, so as to bring us up to the wind. We then soon had the satisfaction of seeing our enemy obliged to take in sail after sail, and a ding-dong race of the most exciting nature right in the wind's eye commenced.

The freshening breeze and rising sea now seemed to increase the odds against our, the smaller, boat, and so critical did matters become, and so certain did capture appear, that I divided between Murray-Aynsley—who was a passenger on this trip,—Steele, and myself sixty sovereigns which I had on board, determined that when captured we wouldn't be penniless. As the weather grew worse we found ourselves obliged to throw overboard our deck cargo in order to lighten the boat. This was done as quickly as possible, heart-breaking though it was to see valuable bales (worth from £50 to £60 apiece) bobbing about on the waves. To me more especially did this come home, for my little private venture of ten bales of Sea Island cotton had to go first, a dead loss of £800 or more!

A fresh cause of excitement now arose; in clearing out these very bales, which were in a half finished deck cabin, an unfortunate stowaway came to light, a runaway slave, who must have been standing wedged between two bales for at least forty-eight hours, and within three feet of whom I had unconsciously been sleeping on the cotton bales during the last two nights before putting to sea. He received a great ovation on our landing him at Nassau, though his freedom cost us $4000 on our return to Wilmington, this being what he was valued at. His escape was an unusual one, for, before leaving port the hold and closed up spaces were always fumigated to such an extent as to have brought out or suffocated any one in hiding; but this being an open-deck cabin, the precaution was impossible.

Having got rid of our deck cargo, we slowly but steadily began to gain in the race. It was an extraordinary sight to see our gallant little vessel at times almost submerged by green seas sweeping her fore and aft, and the *James Adger*,

a vessel of 2000 tons, taking headers into the
huge waves, yet neither of us for a moment
slackening speed, a course we should have
thought madness under ordinary circumstances.
Murray-Aynsley stood with his sextant, taking
angles, and reporting now one now the other
vessel getting the best of it.

Suddenly a fresh danger arose from the
bearings of the engines becoming heated, owing
to the enormous strain put upon them. Erskine
said it was absolutely imperative to stop for
a short time. But by dint of loosening the
bearings and applying all the salad oil procurable mixed with gunpowder they were gradually
got into working order again, all in the engine-
room having assisted in the most energetic
manner at this crucial moment.

The chase went on for fifteen weary hours—
the longest hours I think I ever spent !—until
nightfall, when we saw our friend, then only
about five miles astern, turn round and relin-
quish her pursuit. We heard afterwards that
her stokers were dead beat. For some time we
pursued our course, thinking this might be only
a ruse on their part, and then held a council of

war as to our next move. Steele and Erskine
were for making Bermuda, as we had been
chased 150 miles in that direction, and
both feared our coal would not hold out for
us to reach Nassau. It was, however, very
necessary that I should go to the latter place, as
I was expecting two new steamers out from
England, so we decided to make the attempt.
We only succeeded in reaching land at all by a
very close shave. At the end of the third day
we saw our last coal used ; mainmast, bulwarks,
deck cabin and every available bit of wood,
supplemented by cotton and turpentine as fuel,
only just carried us into one of the north-east
keys of the Bahamas, about sixty miles from
Nassau, into which we absolutely crawled, the
engines working almost on a vacuum. We had
not anchored there more than two hours when
we saw a Northern cruiser steam slowly past,
evidently eyeing us greedily ; but we were safe
in British territory, and even the audacious
cruiser dare not take us as a prize.

The difficulty of procuring the necessary
fuel, in order to take us to Nassau, now
presented itself; fortunately we spied out a

schooner in the neighbourhood with whom we communicated, and after some negotiations I arranged that she should take Murray-Aynsley and myself to our destination, and bring back a cargo of coal.

We started with a fair wind, but before long this had changed to a regular hurricane —during which it was impossible to keep on any sail, and the crew became terrified and helpless, thereby very nearly letting us drift on to the rocks near Abaco lighthouse. It was an awful night, the lightning vivid, and the coast line not many yards away. The crew became more and more demoralised, and when the weather moderated refused to proceed. This new difficulty was only overcome by Murray - Aynsley and myself producing our revolvers; then, partly by threats, and partly by promised bribes, we prevailed on them to think better of their resolve.

Utterly wearied out, having had no sleep to speak of for one week, and having lived in our sea-boots since we made our first start from Wilmington (my feet were so swollen that the boots had to be cut off, and sleeping draughts at first were powerless to restore the lost faculty), we finally arrived in safety. The schooner was despatched back with coal, and three days later I had the satisfaction of seeing the *Banshee* after these hair-breadth escapes steam safely in, though looking considerably dilapidated ; lucky in having lost only our deck cargo—which represented a good half, or more, of what she started with.

This chase, which lasted fifteen hours, and covered nearly 200 miles, was considered one of the most notable incidents connected with blockade-running during the war, and we heard a good deal about it afterwards. At the time we had been struck by the fact of the *James Adger* not opening fire on us, when so close. The explanation was, that she had no "bow-chasers," and was so certain of capturing us eventually, that she did not think it worth while to "yaw" and fire her broadside guns, and as the weather was so bad she did not care to cast them loose.

This is the last trip I made in the *Banshee* on which anything of note occurred. She made eight round trips in all, and I then left her.

She was captured on the ninth, after another long chase off Cape Hatteras, her captain and crew being taken to Fort Lafayette, where they were detained for about eight months as prisoners in a casemate, badly fed and clothed, and of course overcrowded. Steele spent some weeks in Ludlow Street gaol; when he was released he found, to his delight, that another boat had been built expressly for him, which was christened *Banshee* No. 2.

Some idea of the vast profits accruing from blockade-running at this time can be gathered from the fact that, notwithstanding the total loss of the *Banshee* by capture, she earned sufficient on the eight successful round trips which she made to pay her shareholders 700 per cent on their investment.

Her captors turned her into a gunboat; and we heard afterwards that she had proved anything but a success, being much too tender. Moreover her engines, as we knew, were very hard to manipulate, so much so that on one occasion it was found impossible to stop her, and she ran right into the jetty of the naval yard at Washington.

CHAPTER VII

LIFE AT NASSAU

Society at Nassau—Dinners and dancing—The only frock-coat in Nassau—Mrs. Bayley's receptions—Arthur Doering—Old friends who have gone—Hobart Pasha—Capture of the *Don*—Hugh Burgoyne—Captain Hewett—Murray-Aynsley—A private Joint Stock Company—Increased responsibilites—A day's misfortunes—Career of the *Tristram Shandy*—Yellow Jack—Death-rate at Wilmington —Saved from quarantine by a horse—A pet game-cock.

As the moon was now approaching full, we had ample time to repair damages and refit ship before making another start, and we all enjoyed our brief holiday and freedom from care. Although Nassau was a small place its gaieties were many and varied. Money flowed like water, men lived for the day and never thought of the morrow, and in that small place was accumulated a mixture of mankind seldom seen before. Confederate military and naval officers; diplomatists using the blockade-runners as a means of ingress and egress

from their beleaguered country; newspaper
correspondents and advertisers of all kinds,—
some rascals no doubt; the very cream of the
English navy, composed of officers on half-
pay who had come out lured by the prospects
of making some money and gaining an experience in their profession which a war such as
this could give them; and last but not least our
own immediate circle, which was graced by the
presence of two ladies, Mrs. Murray-Aynsley
and Mrs. Hobart, wives of officers who pre-
sided at our revels and tended to keep the
younger and more reckless of our set in order.

What jovial days they were, and how they
were appreciated by the officials and natives, to
whom it was a pleasure to extend our hospitality. Every night our dinner table was filled to
its utmost capacity, and once a week at least
we had a dance, when the office furniture was
unceremoniously bundled out into the garden
under the care of a fatigue party of soldiers,
and the band of the regiment discoursed en-
trancing music to those whose feet never
seemed to tire. I suppose that I was then
rather a dandy and the only possessor of a

frock-coat among us, and as I lived just below
Government House, this coat, with a flower in
the button-hole, was frequently requisitioned at
Mrs. Bayley's (the Governor's wife) receptions.
I have known it do duty half a dozen times on
half a dozen backs within a couple of hours :
in the case of poor Vizitelly, however, it was a
little wanting in front.

Not only my coat became public property,
but those gay friends parted my other raiment
between them, and I well remember, after I
had a new supply of linen, etc. from home, ex-
postulating with Frankston, my black major-
domo, because I had nothing to wear, and
receiving his answer in reply—" Well, sar, what
can do? Mr. Hurst and Mr. Doering take all
master's shirts." To back up his assertion, he
showed me Arthur Doering's weekly wash just
arrived, consisting of one sock and one white
tie. Poor Arthur, he is gone,—a light-hearted,
cheery, devil-may-care youngster who spent
every penny he made. He was one of my
pursers, but had persistently bad luck ; he was
captured twice, wrecked once, and chased back
once. When on shore I made him head of the

entertaining department, for which he was well fitted, as no one could mix a better cocktail or sing a more cheery song than he could.

This was the cheery side of our Nassau life, but it had its reverse one, consisting of hard work, constant anxieties and worries.

As my memory takes me back to those jovial but hard-working days of "camaraderie" it is melancholy to think how many of those friends have gone before: Mrs. Murray-Aynsley, Mrs. Hobart and her husband Hobart Pasha; Hugh Burgoyne, one of the navy's brightest ornaments, who was drowned while commanding the ill-fated *Captain;* Hewett, who lately gave up command of the Channel Fleet only to die; old Steele, the king of blockade-running captains; Maurice Portman, an ex-diplomatist; Frank Vizitelly, whose bones lie alongside those of Hicks Pasha's in the Soudan; Lewis Grant Watson, my brother agent; Arthur Doering, one of my loyal lieutenants, and a host of old Confederate friends, are all gone, and I could count on my fingers those remaining of a circle of chums who did not know what care or fear was, and who would have stood by each other through thick and thin in any emergency. In fact my old friends Admiral Murray-Aynsley and Frank Hurst are almost the only two living of that companionship.

Of Hobart Pasha and of the important part he played in the Turko-Russian war and Cretan rebellion—in which he acknowledged that his blockade-running experiences stood him in such good stead—most, if not all, my readers will have read or heard. He commanded a smart little twin screw-steamer called the *Don*, in fact one of the first twin propeller steamers ever built. And very proud he was of his craft, in which he made several successful runs under the assumed name of Captain Roberts. On her first trip after "Captain Roberts" gave up command in order to go home, the *Don* was captured after a long chase, and his late chief officer, who was then in charge, was assumed by his captors to be Roberts. He maintained silence concerning the point, and the Northern newspapers upon the arrival of the prize at Philadelphia were full of the subject of the "Capture of the *Don* and the notorious

English naval officer, Captain Roberts." Much chagrined were they to find they had got the wrong man, and that the English naval officer was still at large.

Poor Burgoyne—whose tragic and early end, owing to the capsizing of the *Captain*, everybody deplored—as a blockade-runner was not very successful. If I remember correctly he made only two or three trips. Had he lived he would have had a brilliant career before him in the navy; bravest of the brave, as is evidenced by the V.C. he wore, gentle as a woman, unselfish to a fault, he might have saved his life if he had thought more of himself and less of his men on that terrible occasion off Finisterre, when his last words were, " Look out for yourselves, men ; never mind me."

Then there was Hewett, another wearer of the "cross for valour," who has only recently joined the majority, after a brilliant career as Admiral commanding in the East Indies, Red Sea, and Channel Fleet ; who successfully interviewed King John in Abyssinia, and was not content to pace the deck of his flagship at Suakim, but insisted upon fighting in the square at El Teb, and whose hospitality and geniality later on as Commander-in-Chief of the Channel Fleet was proverbial.

Murray-Aynsley, I rejoice to say, is still alive. Who that knows "old Murray" does not love him ; gentle as a child, brave as a lion, a man without guile, he was perhaps the most successful of all the naval blockade-runners. In the *Venus* he had many hair-breadth escapes, notably on one occasion when he ran the gauntlet of the Northern Fleet in daylight into Wilmington. The *Venus*, hotly pursued by several blockaders and pounded at by others, straight through whom she steamed, and old Murray on the bridge, with his coat sleeves hitched up almost to his arm-pits—a trick he had when greatly excited—otherwise as cool as possible, was, as Lamb afterwards told me, a sight not to be forgotten.

But shore life in Nassau was by no means "all beer and skittles." As I have stated, the cheery side had its reverse. So far as I was concerned, I had always a busy time attending to the mercantile part of the business, and latterly a large staff of clerks, captains, and

officers to supervise, to manage whom required
all the tact and firmness of which as a comparative youngster I was capable. But on
the whole they were a loyal set of men ; some
imbeciles were indeed sent out as captains,
who were no more fit to command a blockade-
runner than I was a regiment, and these men
had to be superseded and replaced by others :
which caused much friction, but the interests
involved were so large that I could not afford to
be sentimental.

The business had now grown to very large
proportions ; owing to the success achieved
by the first *Banshee* her shareholders were
encouraged to make further investments, and
their friends were only too delighted to follow
suit. The consequence was that my principals
at home established a private Joint Stock
Company with a large capital, by means of
which steamer after steamer was built and
sent out for me to manipulate.

Individual ventures gradually became the
exception, and on account of the amount of
capital required it was found more profitable
to form large companies. The risk of loss

was lessened by the possession of a greater number of vessels, as even if half the fleet owned by a company were captured the profits earned by the other half would more than counterbalance the loss entailed by failure. The mercantile house which transacted the company's business invariably held a large quantity of the stock, and the commission earned was so great that, even if the individual stockholders lost, the mercantile house came out a gainer.

This change increased immensely my responsibilities and anxieties ; vast sums had to be dealt with, and at times a decision had to be made in an instant upon a subject which involved grave consequences but brooked little delay. However, youth and a sanguine temperament seemed to carry me along, and in those days I managed to brush aside difficulties and annoyances which in these later times would appear to me insufferable.

One morning I was wakened up at daylight by Doering and the captain of a boat called the *Tristram Shandy*, which I had despatched only five days before on her maiden trip, standing at the foot of my bed. They explained to me that they had arrived within 100 miles of Wilmington when they had fallen in with a fast cruiser, who had chased them; to avoid capture they had been obliged to throw all their cargo overboard. This in itself meant a serious loss, but it was not the sum-total of the day's misfortunes, for some hours later I heard of the capture of another of our boats, and the total destruction of a third by being run ashore and destroyed by the blockaders—a heavy bill of misfortune for one day!

The *Tristram Shandy* had a very short and unfortunate career; after being reloaded subsequent to her compulsory return, she started on her second attempt and steamed safely in. But in coming out her funnels, owing to the peculiar construction of her boilers, flamed very much, and it appears that a gunboat followed her by this flame all night, and when morning broke was seen to be about three miles astern. The captain at once ordered extra steam to be put on, but owing to this having been done too suddenly, one of her valve spindles was wrenched off, and she lay helpless at the mercy of the chaser, who speedily came up and took possession.

She had on board a very valuable cargo of cotton, and in addition $50,000 in specie belonging to the Confederate Government; this, according to agreement with the Government, Doering proceeded to throw overboard, but some of the crew, determined to have a finger in the spoil, rushed aft and broke open the kegs. In the mêlée a quantity of gold pieces were strewn among the cotton bales on deck, and when the Northerners came on board they were very irate to think they had lost a considerable portion of their prize money. The steamer was taken into Philadelphia and condemned, and the crew were kept prisoners in New York for several months.

In addition to the worries and anxieties I have detailed we had to fight that demon, yellow Jack, which raged with fearful mortality both at Nassau and Wilmington. In Nassau I have counted seventeen funerals pass my house before breakfast, and in one day I have attended interments of three intimate friends. In Wilmington it was worse; in one season alone, out of a total population of 6000, 2500 died. No wonder the authorities were scared and imposed heavy penalties on us in the shape of quarantine. On two occasions I have been in quarantine for fifty days at a time—think of that, *you* modern luxurious travellers, who growl if *you* are detained three days.

On the first occasion out of a crew of thirty-two twenty-eight were laid low, and we had seven deaths; only the captain, chief engineer, steward, and myself were free from fever. On the second we had no sickness, and only suffered from the ennui consequent upon such close confinement and short rations, as latterly we had nothing but salt pork and sardines to eat. We were only saved from a third dose of quarantine almost by a miracle.

It happened that the Southern Agent in Egypt had sent a very valuable Arab horse to Nassau, as a present for Jefferson Davis. Heiliger, the Confederate Agent there, asked me if I would take it in through the blockade.

H

I at once consented, and it was shipped on
board the *Banshee*. We got through all
right, but when the health officer came on
board and ordered us to quarantine, I said:
"If we have to go there, the horse will
certainly have to be destroyed, as we have
no food for it." Thereupon he telegraphed
to Richmond, and the reply came back that
the *Banshee* was to proceed to the town,
land the horse, and return to quarantine.
When we were alongside the wharf a large
number of our crew jumped on shore and
disappeared. I said to the General, who was
a friend of mine, "It is no use our going
back to quarantine after this, you either have
the infection or not," and I induced him to
telegraph again to Richmond. The answer
came back, "*Banshee* must discharge and
load as quickly as possible, and proceed to
sea; lend all assistance."

The General acted on these instructions,
and upon the third day we were gaily pro-
ceeding down the river again with an outward
cargo on board, passing quite a fleet of
steamers at the quarantine ground, whose

crews were gnashing their teeth. We got safely out and returned, after making another trip, to find the same boats in quarantine, and, as it was raised some three days after our arrival, we steamed up the river in company, much to the disgust of their crews.

Good old horse, he saved me from a dreary confinement in quarantine, and made the owners of the *Banshee* some £20,000 to £30,000 extra, but he was nearly the cause of our all being put in a Northern prison and losing our steamer. On a very still night, as we were running in and creeping noiselessly through the hostile fleet, he commenced neighing (smelling the land, I expect). In an instant two or three jackets were thrown over his head; but it was too late; he had been heard on board a cruiser very close to which we were passing, and she and two or three of her consorts immediately opened fire upon us. We had the heels of them, however, and our friend Colonel Lamb at Fort Fisher was soon protecting us, playing over our heads with shell.

On a subsequent occasion disaster might

have overtaken the *Banshee* under somewhat similar circumstances had a cruiser happened to be near. A game-cock which we kept on board as a pet suddenly began to crow. But this time the disaster was to the game-cock and not to the *Banshee*, for, pet as he was, his neck was promptly twisted. Such experiences as these showed how easy it was to increase the risks of blockade-running; absence of all avoidable noise at night was as essential as the extinction of all lights on board ship.

CHAPTER VIII

OUR FLEET

THE reason for my leaving the *Banshee* was the arrival at Nassau of a new steamer which my firm had sent out to me. This was the *Will-o'-the-Wisp*, and great things were expected from her. She was built on the Clyde, was a much larger and faster boat than the *Banshee*, but shamefully put together, and most fragile. My first introduction to her was seeing her appear off Nassau, and receiving a message by the pilot boat, from Capper, the captain, to say that the vessel was leaking badly and he dare not stop his engines, as they had to be kept going in order to work the pumps. We brought her into the harbour, and having beached her and afterwards made all necessary repairs on the slipway, I decided to take a trip in her.

As soon as the nights were sufficiently dark we made a start for Wilmington, unfortunately meeting very bad weather and strong head winds, which delayed us; the result was that instead of making out the blockading fleet about midnight, as we had intended, when dawn was breaking there were still no signs of them. Capper, the chief engineer, and I then held a hurried consultation as to what we had better do. Capper was for going to sea again, and if necessary returning to Nassau; the weather was still threatening, our coal supply running short, and, with a leaky ship beneath us, the engineer and I decided that the lesser risk would be to make a dash for it. "All right," said Capper, "we'll go on, but you'll get d——d well peppered!"

We steamed cautiously on, making as little smoke as possible, whilst I went to the mast-

head to take a look round : no land was in
sight, but I could make out in the dull morning
light the heavy spars of the blockading flagship
right ahead of us, and soon after several other
masts became visible on each side of her.
Picking out what appeared to me to be the
widest space between these, I signalled to
the deck how to steer, and we went steadily
on—determined when we found we were
perceived to make a rush for it. No doubt
our very audacity helped us through, as for
some time they took no notice, evidently
thinking we were one of their own chasers
returning from sea to take up her station for
the day.

At last, to my great relief, I saw Fort
Fisher just appearing above the horizon,
although we knew that the perilous passage
between these blockaders must be made
before we could come under the friendly
protection of its guns. Suddenly, we became
aware that our enemy had found us out ; we
saw two cruisers steaming towards one another
from either side of us, so as to intercept us
at a given point before we could get on the

land side of them. It now became simply a question of speed and immunity from being sunk by shot. Our little vessel quivered again under the tremendous pressure with which she was being driven through the water.

An exciting time followed, as we and our two enemies rapidly converged upon one point, others in the distance also hurrying up to assist them. We were now near enough to be within range, and the cruiser on our port side opened fire; his first shot carried away our flagstaff aft on which our ensign had just been hoisted; his second tore through our forehold, bulging out a plate on the opposite side. Bedding and blankets to stop the leak were at once requisitioned, and we steamed on full speed under a heavy fire from both quarters. Suddenly, puffs of smoke from the fort showed us that Colonel Lamb, the commandant, was aware of what was going on and was firing to protect us; a welcome proof that we were drawing within range of his guns and on the landward side of our pursuers, who, after giving us a few more parting shots, hauled off and steamed away from within reach

of the shells which we were rejoiced to see
falling thickly around them.

We had passed through a most thrilling
experience; at one time the cruiser on our
port side was only a hundred yards with her
consort a hundred and fifty away from us on
the starboard, and it seemed a miracle that
their double fire had not completely sunk us.
It certainly required all one's nerve to stand
upon the paddle-box, looking without flinching
almost into the muzzles of the guns, which
were firing at us; and proud we were of our
crew, not a man of whom showed the white
feather. Our pilot, who showed no lack of
courage at the time, became, however, terribly
excited as we neared the bar, and whether it
was that the ship steered badly, owing to
being submerged forward, or from some
mistake, he ran her ashore whilst going at
full speed. The result was a most frightful
shaking, which of course materially increased
the leaks, and we feared she would become a
total wreck; fortunately the tide was rising,
and, through lightening her by throwing some
of the cargo overboard, we succeeded in getting

her off and steamed up the river to Wilmington, where we placed her on the mud.

After repairing the shot holes and other damage, we were under the impression that no further harm from running ashore had come to her, as all leaks were apparently stopped and the ship was quite tight. The result proved us to be sadly wrong on this point. After loading our usual cargo we started down the river all right, and waited for nightfall in order to cross the bar and run through the fleet. No sooner had we crossed it and found ourselves surrounded by cruisers than the chief engineer rushed on to the bridge, saying the water was already over the stoke-hole plates, and he feared that the ship was sinking. At the same moment a quantity of firewood which was stowed round one of the funnels (and which was intended to eke out our somewhat scanty coal supply) caught fire, and flames burst out.

This placed us in a pretty predicament, as it showed our whereabouts to two cruisers which were following us, one on each quarter. They at once opened a furious cannonade

HALF-PAST-THE-BUSK'S DASH FOR WILMINGTON.

To face page 136

upon us ; however, although shells were bursting all around and shot flying over us, all
hands worked with a will, and we soon extinguished the flames, which were acting as a
treacherous beacon to our foes. Fortunately
the night was intensely dark, and nothing
could be seen beyond a radius of thirty or
forty yards, so, thanks to this, we were soon
enabled, by altering our helm, to give our
pursuers the slip, whilst they probably kept on
their course.

We had still the other enemy to deal with ;
but our chief engineer and his staff had mean-
while been hard at work and had turned on
the "bilge - injection" and "donkey - pumps."
Still, the leak was gaining upon us, and it
became evident that the severe shaking which
the ship got when run aground had started
the plates in her bottom. The mud had
been sucked up when she lay in the river at
Wilmington, thus temporarily repairing the
damage ; but when she got into the sea-way
the action of the water opened them again.
Even the steam pumps now could not prevent
the water from gradually increasing ; four of

our eight furnaces were extinguished, and the firemen were working up to their middles in water.

It was a critical time when daylight broke, dull and threatening. The captain was at the wheel, and I at the mast-head (all other hands being employed at the pumps, and even baling), when, not four miles off, I sighted a cruiser broadside on. She turned round as if preparing to give chase, and I thought we were done for, as we could not have got more than three or four knots an hour out of our crippled boat. To my great joy, however, I found our alarm was needless, for she evidently had not seen us, and instead of heading turned her stern towards us and disappeared into a thick bank of clouds.

Still we were far from being out of danger, as the weather became worse and worse and the wind increased in force until it was blowing almost a gale. Things began to look as ugly as they could, and even Capper lost hope : I shall never forget the expression on his face as he came up to me and said, in his gruff voice, " I say, Mr. Taylor! the beggar's going, the beggar's going," pointing vehemently downwards. "What the devil do you mean!" I exclaimed. "Why, we are going to lose the ship and our lives too," was the answer. It is not possible for any one unacquainted with Capper to appreciate this scene. Sturdy, thickset, nearly as broad as he was long, and with the gruffest manner but kindest heart,— although a rough diamond and absolutely without fear. With the exception of Steele he was the best blockade-running captain we had.

In order to save the steamer and our lives we decided that desperate remedies must be resorted to, so again the unlucky deck cargo had to be sacrificed. The good effect of this was soon visible; we began to gain on the water, and were able, by degrees, to relight our extinguished fires. But the struggle continued to be a most severe one, for just when we began to obtain a mastery over the water the donkey-engine broke down, and before we could repair it the water increased sensibly, nearly putting out our fires again. So the struggle went on for sixty hours, when we were truly thankful to steam into Nassau harbour and beach the ship. It was a very narrow escape, for within twenty minutes after stopping her engines the vessel had sunk to the level of the water.

I had the *Will-o'-the-Wisp* raised, hauled up on the slip, and repaired at an enormous expense before she was fit again for sea. Subsequently she made several trips, but as I found her a constant source of delay and expenditure I decided to sell her. After having her cobbled up with plenty of putty and paint, I was fortunate enough to open negotiations with some Jews with a view to her purchase. Having settled all preliminaries we arranged for a trial trip,. and after a very sumptuous lunch I proceeded to run her over a measured mile for the benefit of the would-be purchasers. I need scarcely mention that we subjected her machinery to the utmost strain, bottling up steam to a pressure of which our present Board of Trade, with its motherly care for our lives, would express strong disapproval. The log line was whisked merrily over the stern of the *Will-o'-the-Wisp*, with the satisfactory result that she logged

$17\frac{1}{2}$ knots. The Jews were delighted, so was I; and the bargain was clinched. I fear, however, that their joy was short-lived; a few weeks afterwards when attempting to steam into Galveston she was run ashore and destroyed by the Federals. When we ran into that port a few months afterwards in the second *Banshee* we saw her old bones on the beach.

After this I made a trip in a new boat that had just been sent out to me, the *Wild Dayrell*. And a beauty she was, very strong, a perfect sea-boat, and remarkably well engined.

Our voyage in was somewhat exciting, as about three o'clock in the afternoon, while making for the Fort Caswell entrance (not Fort Fisher), we were sighted by a Federal cruiser, who immediately gave chase. We soon found however, that we had the heels of our friend, but it left us the alternative of going out to sea or being chased straight into the jaws of the blockaders off the bar before darkness came on. Under these circumstances what course to take was a delicate point to decide, but we solved the problem by slowing down just sufficiently to keep a few miles ahead of our chaser, hoping that darkness would come on before we made the fleet or they discovered us. Just as twilight was drawing in we made them out ; cautiously we crept on, feeling certain that our friend astern was rapidly closing up on us. Every moment we expected to hear shot whistling around us. So plainly could we see the sleepy blockaders that it seemed almost impossible we should escape their notice. Whether they did not expect a runner to make an attempt so early in the evening, or whether it was sheer good luck on our part, I know not, but we ran through the lot without being seen or without having a shot fired at us.

Our anxieties, however, were not yet over, as our pilot (a new hand) lost his reckoning and put us ashore on the bar. Fortunately the flood tide was rising fast, and we refloated, bumping over stern first in a most inglorious fashion, and anchored off Fort Caswell before 7 P.M.—a record performance. Soon after anchoring and while enjoying the usual cocktail we saw a great commotion among the blockaders, who were throwing up rockets and flashing lights,

evidently in answer to signals from the cruiser
which had so nearly chased us into their midst.

When we came out we met with equally
good luck, as the night was pitch dark and the
weather very squally.   No sooner did we clear
the bar than we put our helm aport, ran down
the coast, and then stood boldly straight out to
sea without interference : and it was perhaps as
well we had such good fortune, as before this
I had discovered that our pilot was of a very
indifferent calibre, and that courage was not our
captain's most prominent characteristic.   The
poor *Wild Dayrell* deserved a better com-
mander, and consequently a better fate than
befell her.   She was lost on her second trip,
entirely through the want of pluck on the part
of her captain, who ran her ashore some miles
to the north of Fort Fisher ; as *he* said in order
to avoid capture,—to my mind a fatal excuse for
any blockade-running captain to make.   'Twere
far better to be sunk by shot and escape in the
boats if possible.   I am quite certain that if
Steele had commanded her on that trip she would
never have been put ashore, and the chances
are that she would have come through all right.

I

I never forgave myself for not unshipping the captain on my return to Nassau ; my only excuse was that there was no good man available to replace him with, and he was a particular protégé of my chiefs. But such considerations should not have weighed, and if I had had the courage of my convictions it is probable the *Wild Dayrell* would have proved as successful as any of our steamers.

About this time I had two other new boats sent out, the *Stormy Petrel* and the *Wild Rover*, both good boats, very fast, and distinct improvements on the *Banshee* No. 1 and *Will-o'-the-Wisp*. The *Stormy Petrel* had, however, very bad luck, as after getting safely in and anchoring behind Fort Fisher she settled as the tide went down on a submerged anchor, the fluke of which went through her bottom, and despite all efforts she became a total wreck : this was one of the most serious and unlucky losses I had. The *Wild Rover* was more successful, as she made five round trips, on one of which I went in her. She survived the war, and I eventually sent her to South America, where she was sold for a good sum.

CHAPTER IX

BERMUDA

WE had in the early part of the war a depôt at Bermuda as well as at Nassau, and Frank Hurst was at that time my brother agent there. I went there twice, once in the first *Banshee*, and once from Halifax, after a trip to Canada in order to recruit from a bad attack of yellow fever; but I never liked Bermuda, and later on we transferred Hurst and his agency to Nassau, which was more convenient in many ways and nearer Wilmington. Moreover I had to face the contingency, which afterwards occurred, of the Atlantic

ports being closed and our being driven to
the Gulf. The Mudians, however, were a
kind, hospitable lot, and made a great deal
of us, and there was a much larger naval and
military society stationed there than in Nassau.
They had suffered from a severe outbreak of
yellow fever, and the 3rd Buffs, who were in
garrison at the time, had been almost decimated
by it.

It was on my second trip to the island that
one of the finest boats we ever possessed, called
the *Night Hawk*, came out, and I concluded
to run in with her. She was a new side-wheel
steamer of some 600 tons gross, rigged as
a fore and aft schooner, with two funnels,
220 feet long, 21½ feet beam, and 11 feet in
depth ; a capital boat for the work, fast, strong,
of light draught, and a splendid sea-boat—a
great merit in a blockade-runner that sometimes
has to be forced in all weathers. The *Night
Hawk's* career was a very eventful one, and
she passed an unusually lively night off Fort
Fisher on her first attempt.

Soon after getting under weigh our troubles
began. We ran ashore outside Hamilton,

one of the harbours of Bermuda, and hung
on a coral reef for a couple of hours. There
loomed before us the dismal prospect of delay
for repairs, or, still worse, the chance of
springing a leak and experiencing such
difficulties and dangers as we had undergone
on the *Will-o'-the-Wisp*, but fortunately we
came off without damage and were able to
proceed on our voyage.

Another anxiety now engrossed my mind :
the captain was an entirely new hand, and
nearly all the crew were green at the work ;
moreover, the Wilmington pilot was quite
unknown to me, and I could see from the
outset that he was very nervous and badly
wanting in confidence. What would I not
have given for our trusty Tom Burroughs.
However, we had to make the best of it, as,
owing to the demand, the supply of competent
pilots was not nearly sufficient, and towards the
close of the blockade the so-called pilots were
no more than boatmen or men who had been
trading in and out of Wilmington or Charleston
in coasters. Notwithstanding my fears, all
went well on the way across, and the *Night*

Hawk proved to be everything that could be desired in speed and seaworthiness.

We had sighted unusually few craft, and nothing eventful occurred until the third night. Soon after midnight we found ourselves uncomfortably near a large vessel. It was evident that we had been seen, as we heard them beating to quarters and were hailed. We promptly sheered off and went full speed ahead, greeted by a broadside which went across our stern.

When we arrived within striking distance of Wilmington bar the pilot was anxious to go in by Smith's inlet, but as he acknowledged that he knew very little about it I concluded it was better to keep to the new inlet passage, where, at all events, we should have the advantage of our good friend Lamb to protect us ; and I felt that as I myself knew the place so well, this was the safest course to pursue. We were comparatively well through the fleet, although heavily fired at, and arrived near to the bar, passing close by two Northern launches which were lying almost upon it. Unfortunately it was dead low water, and

although I pressed the pilot to give our boat
a turn round, keeping under weigh, and to wait
a while until the tide made, he was so demoralised by the firing we had gone through
and the nearness of the launches, which were
constantly throwing up rockets, that he insisted
upon putting her at the bar, and, as I feared,
we grounded on it forward, and with the
strong flood-tide quickly broached-to, broadside on to the Northern breaker. We kept
our engines going for some time—but to no
purpose, as we found we were only being
forced by the tide more on to the breakers.
Therefore we stopped, and all at once found
our friends, the two launches, close aboard :
they had discovered we were ashore, and had
made up their minds to attack us.

At once all was in confusion ; the pilot and
signalman rushed to the dinghy, lowered it, and
made good their escape ; the captain lost his
head and disappeared ; and the crews of the
launches, after firing several volleys, one of
which slightly wounded me, rowed in to board
us on each sponson. Just at this moment I
suddenly recollected that our private despatches,

which ought to have been thrown overboard,
were still in the starboard life-boat. I rushed
to it, but found the lanyard to which the
sinking weight was attached was foul of one
of the thwarts; I tugged and tugged, but to
no purpose, so I sung out for a knife which
was handed to me by a fireman, and I cut the
line and pitched the bag overboard as the
Northerners jumped on board. Eighteen
months afterwards that fireman accosted me
in the Liverpool streets, saying, " Mr. Taylor,
do you remember my lending you a knife."
" Of course I do," I replied, giving him a tip
at which he was mightily pleased : poor fellow,
he had been thirteen months in a Northern
prison.

When the Northerners jumped on board
they were terribly excited. I don't know
whether they expected resistance or not, but
they acted more like maniacs than sane men,
firing their revolvers and cutting right and left
with their cutlasses. I stood in front of the
men on the poop and said that we surrendered,
but all the reply I received from the lieutenant
commanding was, " Oh, you surrender, do

you ?" . . . accompanied by a string of the choicest Yankee oaths and sundry reflections upon my parentage ; whereupon he fired his revolver twice point blank at me not two yards distant : it was a miracle he did not kill me, as I heard the bullets whiz past my head. This roused my wrath, and I expostulated in the strongest terms upon his firing on unarmed men ; he then cooled down, giving me into the charge of two of his men, one of whom speedily possessed himself of my binoculars. Fortunately, as I had no guard to my watch, they didn't discover it, and I have it still.

Finding they could not get the ship off, and afraid, I presume, of Lamb and his men coming to our rescue, the Federals commenced putting the captain (who had been discovered behind a boat !) and the crew into the boats ; they then set the ship on fire fore and aft, and she soon began to blaze merrily. At this moment one of our firemen, an Irishman, sung out, " Begorra, we shall all be in the air in a minute, the ship is full of gunpowder !" No sooner did the Northern sailors hear this than a panic seized them, and they rushed to their boats, threatening to leave their officers behind if they did not come along. The men who were holding me dropped me like a hot potato, and to my great delight jumped into their boat, and away they rowed as fast as they could, taking all our crew, with the exception of the second officer, one of the engineers, four seamen and myself, as prisoners.

We chuckled at our lucky escape, but we were not out of the wood yet, as we had only a boat half stove in, in which to reach the shore through some 300 yards of surf, and we were afraid at any moment that our enemies finding there was no powder on board might return. We made a feeble effort to put the fire out, but it had gained too much headway, and although I offered the men with me £50 apiece to stand by me and persevere, they were too demoralised and began to lower the shattered boat, swearing that they would leave me behind if I didn't come with them. There was nothing for it but to go, yet the passage through the boiling surf seemed more dangerous to my mind than remaining on the burning ship. The blockaders

immediately opened fire when they knew their
own men had left the *Night Hawk*, and that
she was burning; and Lamb's great shells
hurtling over our heads, and those from the
blockading fleet bursting all around us, formed
a weird picture. In spite of the hail of shot
and shell and the dangers of the boiling surf,
we reached the shore in safety, wet through,
and glad I was in my state of exhaustion from
loss of blood and fatigue to be welcomed by
Lamb's orderly officer.

The poor *Night Hawk* was now a sheet
of flame, and I thought it was all up with her;
and indeed it would have been had it not been
for Lamb, who, calling for volunteers from
his garrison, sent off two or three boat loads
of men to her, and when I came down to the
beach, after having my wound dressed and
a short rest, I was delighted to find the fire
had sensibly decreased. I went on board, and
after some hours of hard work the fire was
extinguished. But what a wreck she was!

Luckily with the rising tide she had bumped
over the bank, and was now lying on the
main beach much more accessible and sheltered.

Still it seemed an almost hopeless task to save
her; but we were not going to be beaten without a try, so, having ascertained how she lay
and the condition she was in, I resolved to
have an attempt to get her dry, and telegraphed
to Wilmington for assistance.

Our agent sent me down about 300
negroes to assist in baling and pumping, and
I set them to work at once. As good luck
would have it, my finest steamer, *Banshee* No.
2, which had just been sent out, ran in the
next night. She was a great improvement on
the first *Banshee*, having a sea-speed of 15½
knots, which was considered very fast in those
days; her length was 252 feet, beam 31 feet,
depth 11 feet, her registered tonnage 439 tons,
and her crew consisted of fifty-three in all. I
at once requisitioned her for aid in the shape
of engineers and men, so that now I had
everything in the way of hands I could want.
Our great difficulty was that the *Night Hawk's*
anchors would not hold for us to get a fair haul
at her.

But here again I was to be in luck. For
the very next night the *Falcon*, commanded

by poor Hewett, in attemping to run in stuck
fast upon the bank over which we had
bumped, not one hundred yards to windward of us, and broke in two. It is an ill
wind that blows nobody good, and Hewett's
mischance proved the saving of our ship.
Now we had a hold for our chain cables by
making them fast to the wreck, and were able
gradually to haul her off by them a little during
each tide, until on the seventh day we had
her afloat in a gut between the bank and the
shore, and at high water we steamed under our
own steam gaily up the river to Wilmington.

Considering the appliances we had and the
circumstances under which we were working,
the saving of that steamer was certainly a
wonderful performance, as we were under
fire almost the whole time. The Northerners,
irritated, no doubt, by their failure to destroy
the ship, used to shell us by day and send in
boats by night; Lamb, however, put a stop
to the latter annoyance by lending us a couple
of companies to defend us, and one night,
when our enemies rowed close up with the
intention of boarding us, they were glad to

sheer off with the loss of a lieutenant and several men. In spite of all the shot and shell by day and the repeated attacks at night, we triumphed in the end, and, after having the *Night Hawk* repaired at a huge cost and getting together a crew, I gave May, a friend of mine, command of her, and he ran her out successfully with a valuable cargo, which made her pay, notwithstanding all her bad luck and the amount spent upon her. Poor May, he was afterwards governor of Perth gaol, and is dead now,—a high-toned, sensitive gentleman, mightily proud of his ship, lame duck as she was.

When she was burning, our utmost efforts were of course directed towards keeping her engine-room and boilers amidships intact, and confining the flames to both ends; in this we were successful, mainly owing to the fact of her having thwart-ship bunkers : but as regards the rest of the steamer she was a complete wreck; her sides were all corrugated with the heat, and her stern so twisted that her starboard quarter was some two feet higher than her port one, and not a particle of wood-

work was left unconsumed. Owing to the
limited resources of Wilmington as regards
repairs, I found it impossible to have this put
right, so her sides were left as they were, and
the new deck put on on the slope I have
described, and caulked with cotton, as no
oakum was procurable. When completed she
certainly was a queer-looking craft, but as tight
as a bottle and as seaworthy as ever, although
I doubt if any Lloyd's surveyor would have
passed her. But as a matter of fact she came
across the Atlantic, deeply immersed with her
coal supply, through some very bad weather,
without damage, and was sold for a mere
song, to be repaired and made into a passenger
boat for service on the East Coast, where she
ran for many years with success.

It had been a hard week for me, as I had
no clothes except what I had on when we
were boarded,—my servant very cleverly, as
he imagined, having thrown my portmanteau
into the man-of-war's boat when he thought
I was going to be captured, and all I had in
the world was the old serge suit in which I
stood. Being without a change and wet

through every day and night for six days consecutively, it is little wonder that I caught fever and ague, of which I nearly died in Richmond, and which distressing complaint stuck to me for more than eighteen months. I shall never forget, on going to a store in Wilmington for a new rig-out (which by the bye cost $1200), the look of horror on the storekeeper's face when I told him the coat I had purchased would do if he cut a foot off it : he thought it such a waste of expensive material.

A very unfortunate occurrence took place incident upon the wreck of the *Falcon.* She had on board as passenger a Mrs. Greenhow, a famous Confederate spy, who, when the steamer struck, pleaded hard to be put ashore, fearing no doubt capture by the Federals. Hewett was most energetic in his efforts to dissuade her, but at last manned a boat for her, which was upset in the breakers, and she alone was drowned. It was I who found her body on the beach at daylight, and afterwards took it up to Wilmington. A remarkably handsome woman she was, with features which showed much character. Although one cannot

altogether admire the profession of a spy, still
there was no doubt that she imagined herself
in following such a profession to be serving
her country in the only way open to her.

Surely in war the feelings of both men and
women become blunted as to the niceties of
what is right or wrong. I well remember on
one occasion an eminent Confederate officer
bringing me an infernal machine which he
had invented, a kind of shell exactly like
a lump of coal, with a request that some
should be placed on each of our steamers,
and that, in case of capture, they should be
put in the coal bunkers so as to be thrown
into the furnaces by the prize crew. I told
him that this was not my idea of making war,
and moreover mildly suggested that, even if
it were, he seemed to have forgotten that
our crew would probably be on board as
prisoners and be blown up into the air with
their captors.

Another eminent Confederate military doctor
proposed to me during the prevalence of the
yellow fever epidemic that he should ship
by our boats to Nassau and Bermuda sundry

K

cases of infected clothing, which were to be
sent to the North with the idea of spreading
the disease there. This was too much, and
I shouted at him, not in the choicest language,
to leave the office. It is difficult to conceive
of such a diabolical idea, not only to spread
havoc among combatants, but among innocent
women and children, being present in an
educated man's mind.

CHAPTER X

EXPERIENCES ASHORE IN DIXIE'S LAND

Railway travelling in the Southern States—The conductor's car—
Carrying despatches—A weary and anxious wait—Under fire in
a train—Excitement in Richmond—General Lee's headquarter
staff—The Confederate Government—Privations in Richmond—
The bitterest rebels of the war—A startling dinner bill—Pro-
visioning General Lee's army—Admiral Porter's first attack on
Fort Fisher—The *Banshee* No. 2 runs through the Federal Fleet
—General and Mrs. Randolph—A magnificent cargo.

THE dangers and discomforts at sea were not
the only excitements which a blockade-runner
experienced. As the blockade-running fleet
of which I had charge extended, not only
was an increase in my office staff in Nassau
entailed, but a good deal of travelling by rail
to and fro between Wilmington and Richmond,
for the purpose of negotiations with the heads
of departments there regarding the contracts
we had with them, and upon various other
matters.

These trips involved an enormous amount
of fatigue, worry, excitement, and even danger,
as it was no easy matter latterly to get in and
out of the beleaguered city safely ; the railway
journey itself, which often extended over a
couple of days and nights, was an affair of
great discomfort, the permanent way being
anything but permanent, and the rolling stock
too often rolling elsewhere than upon the
rails.   It was considered a joke in those days
to assert that a journey from Wilmington to
Richmond was almost as dangerous as an
engagement with the enemy.   The only place
on the train where any approach to comfort
was obtainable was in the conductor's car,
the entrée to which I generally contrived to
secure, aided by a little judicious palm-greas-
ing and the possession of a brandy bottle or
two ; but the latter had its disadvantages, as
the word was soon passed round that there
was a Britisher on board the train with some
real good brandy.   And it was considered the
duty of every one to whom I had stood a drink
to introduce a friend who wanted one badly ;
consequently the brandy was generally used up

on the outward trip, and there was little left
for the return.   But it was great pleasure to
be able to quench the poor fellows' thirst,
more especially the wounded, with whom the
cars were often filled to overflowing.

As a rule my good friend Heiliger, Confederate Agent at Nassau, used to entrust me
with despatches, the carriage of which provided me with a pass which much facilitated
my journeys ; but on one occasion towards
the end of the war the possession of these
despatches made it a little awkward for me.
I had arrived one afternoon at Petersburg,
which is about fifteen miles from Richmond,
and found a tremendous hubbub going on.
Butler, having attacked the place with his
corps, hoped to take it and then turn the
Confederate flank.   Although it was but
poorly defended, being held by some 1500
recruits and boys, they kept their ground,
entrenched about a mile outside the town.

It was while this first attack was in progress
that I arrived on the scene, and recognising
the gravity of the position, if the place were
taken and despatches found upon me (an

Englishman), I went to the Commissary-General and asked him to provide me with a horse to take me to Richmond. He said this was impossible, but that they had telegraphed for reinforcements, and that Hoke's division was expected by train in an hour or two, and I had better go to the depôt and there wait my chance of getting the empty return train. It was a weary and anxious wait, as we could hear the attack going on and feared the defence would every moment be overpowered. However, a short time before daylight we heard the train approaching, and soon afterwards it steamed in, crowded even on the roofs of carriages by Hoke's men, who were promptly detrained and hurried off at the double to the scene of action—a welcome reinforcement. I got in the train, and we started for Richmond. We had only proceeded a few miles when, in the gray dawn, we saw a body of Butler's cavalry galloping as hard as they could to intercept us and tear up the line in front. Our engineer, however, equal to the occasion, put on full steam, and we just managed to get ahead of them. Seeing they were too late, they drew up alongside the track and potted at us with their carbines, without, however, wounding any one. They then at once tore up the rails in our rear.

Being under fire in a train was a curious experience, and perhaps more exciting for me than the others, as I had my hand on the blessed despatches, uncertain what to do. Fortunately we arrived safely at Richmond, and I was very glad to be rid of my responsibilities. This was the last train that got in on the direct Wilmington line; after that, in order to get in and out, we had to make a long detour viâ Danville.

I found Richmond in a great state of excitement; the Northern attack had become more animated; the investment was more stringent; the booming of heavy guns was heard night and day; and hourly reports were brought from the front. It was upon this visit that I accompanied Lee's Head-quarter staff on the celebrated march along the south side of the James river, when he marched rapidly to Petersburg in order to confront the Northerners' sudden change of

front on that town.   Upon a previous occasion I had made the acquaintance of the
great General, and on this one I breakfasted
with him.   Shortly afterwards the march,
which was very exciting, began.   We were
constantly in close touch with the enemy,—at
one time marching through the woods, which
were being shelled by the Northern gunboats
in the James river—at another time skirmishing
at close quarters with the Federals' flank ; but
as I had seen most of the seven days' fighting
round Richmond I felt almost an old campaigner.
It was a hard day, as, after being fifteen hours
in the saddle without food, I was obliged to
return to Richmond on important business that
night, instead of bivouacking with the Headquarters staff, as I was pressed to do.   Wearied
and almost exhausted I found on my arrival in
the city that all I could obtain at the hotel was
some corn bread and cold bacon washed down
with water.

The following is an extract from a letter
dated 15th January 1865, written to my chiefs
after this visit to Richmond.

Altogether I think the Confederate Government is going

to the *bad*, and if they don't take care the Confederacy will go too.   I never saw things look so gloomy, and I think spring will finish them unless they make a change for the better.   Georgia is gone, and they say Sherman is going to seize Branchville; if he does, Charleston and Wilmington will be done—and if Wilmington goes Lee has to evacuate Richmond and retire into Tennessee.   He told me the other day, that if they did not keep Wilmington he could not save Richmond.   They nearly had Fort Fisher —they were within sixty yards of it—and had they pushed on as they ought to have done could have taken it.   It was a terrific bombardment; they estimate that about 40,000 shells were sent into it.   Colonel Lamb behaved like a brick—splendidly.   I got the last of the Whitworths in, and they are now at the Fort.   They are very hard up for food in the field, but the *Banshee* has this time 600 barrels of pork and 1500 boxes of meat—enough to feed Lee's army for a month.

The above extract is interesting, as it showed that my diagnosis of the position of affairs, written in January 1865, proved correct as to what actually happened two or three months later.   Sherman *did* capture Branchville, and in consequence Charleston and Wilmington.   When the latter port fell Lee *was* forced to evacuate Richmond and retire towards Tennessee and eventually capitulate. Had Charleston and Wilmington been retained and blockade-running encouraged, instead of having obstacles thrown in the way, I am

convinced that the condition of affairs would
have been altered very materially, and perhaps
would have led to the South obtaining what
it had shed so much blood to gain, viz. its
independence. No doubt at that critical time
the North was making its last supreme effort,
and, had it failed, negotiations would probably
have been opened up with a view to peace.

The privations of the regular residents
in Richmond in those days were very great,
as food of all kinds was very expensive; but
all bore their troubles without a murmur, and
I think there was more enthusiam displayed
there than in any other city in the South;
probably because the people, with the enemy
at their gates, were always in close touch with
them, and also because there was such a large
female element in society there, for the ladies
of the South were proverbially the staunchest
and bitterest rebels of the war. Of course
money still purchased most things, and we
blockade-runners, who were well supplied with
coin, managed to live in comparative comfort
and at times even fared sumptuously. I
remember a great dinner I gave to a few

heads of departments; it was a banquet no
one need have been ashamed of. But oh the
bill!—a little over $5000 (Confederate) for a
dinner to fourteen. When one has to pay
$150 a bottle for champagne, $120 for sherry
or madeira, and as much in proportion for the
viands, the account soon runs up. However,
it was a great success, and well worth the cost.

That morning I had met by appointment
the Commissary-General, who divulged to
me under promise of secrecy that Lee's army
was in terrible straits, and had in fact rations
only for about thirty days. He asked me
if I could help him; I said I would do my
best, and after some negotiations he undertook to pay me a profit of 350 per cent
upon any provisions and meat I could bring
in within the next three weeks! I had then,
discharging in Wilmington, the *Banshee* No.
2, which had just been sent out to replace
the first *Banshee*, and in which I had run the
blockade inwards. I telegraphed instructions
to have her made ready for sea with all speed
and await my arrival. After a somewhat exciting and lengthy journey of three days and

nights, owing to having to go round by Danville, I reached Wilmington, successfully ran
the blockade out, purchased my cargo of provisions, etc. at Nassau for about £6000 (for
which eventually I was paid over £27,000),
and, after a most exciting run in, landed the
same in Wilmington within eighteen days after
leaving Richmond.

In the interim between our leaving Wilmington and our return, Porter's fleet had
made an unsuccessful attack upon Fort Fisher,
and he was just then at the time of our appear-
ance upon the scene concluding his attack and
re-embarking his beaten troops. When morning
broke and we were near the fort we counted
sixty-four vessels that we had passed through.
After being heavily fired into at daybreak by
several gunboats (the fort being unable to
protect us as usual, owing to nearly all its
guns having been put out of action in the
attack of the two previous days), it was an
exciting moment as we crossed the bar in
safety, cheered by the garrison, some 2000
strong, who knew we had provisions on board
for the relief of their comrades in Virginia.

I wrote under date of 15th January 1865 to my chiefs at home with reference to this trip :

I went over in the *Banshee* and had an exciting time of it; we arrived off the bar when Porter's vast fleet was there, and I think the Confederate Trading Company ought to be proud of their two vessels (*Banshee* and *Wild Rover*) both running through that immense fleet and getting safely in.   The *Banshee* was out in front of them all for half an hour after daylight, as we were rather late and could not get up to the bar before.   They said at Fort Fisher that it was a beautiful sight to see the little *Banshee* manœuvring in front of the whole fleet.   They sent some vessels in to pepper us, but every shot missed, and we got in safely. Porter's fleet left that evening, and I think they have given up the attack for a time.

I shall never forget that trip. We sailed from Nassau at dusk on the evening before Christmas day, but were only just outside the harbour when our steam pipe split and we had to return. As it was hopeless on account of the moon to make the attempt unless we could get away next day, I was in despair and thought it was all up with my 350 per cent profit. After long trying in vain to find some one to undertake the necessary repairs, owing to its being Christmas day, I found at last a Yankee, who said : " Well *sir*, its only a question of price."   I said " Name yours," and he replied

"Well I guess $400 for three clamps would be fair." I said "All right, if finished by six o'clock": he set to work, and we made all arrangements to start. Shortly after six the work was finished, but the black pilot then declared he couldn't take her out until the tide turned, there being no room to turn her in the harbour. As it was a question of hours I said, "Back her out." He grinned and said, "Perhaps do plenty damage." "Never mind," said I, "try it"—and we did, with the result that we came plump into the man-of-war lying at the entrance of the harbour (officers all on deck ready to go down to their Christmas dinner), and ground along her side, smashing two of her boats in, but doing ourselves little damage. "Good-bye," I shouted; "a merry Christmas; send the bill in for the boats." Away we went clear, and fortunate it was we did so, as we only arrived off Wilmington just in time to run through Porter's fleet before daybreak.

The trip out was equally exciting, as I had as passengers General Randolph, ex-Secretary of State for War, who was going to Europe invalided, and his wife. I did not want

to take them, as the *Banshee* had practically
no accommodation whatever, particularly for
ladies. However, *she* had such a good
character for safety, that they pleaded hard
to be taken, and I at last consented, though
I did not like at all the responsibility of
having a lady on board. I was determined,
however, to make Mrs. Randolph as safe as
possible, so told the stevedore to keep a square
space between the cotton bales on deck, into
which she could retire in case the firing became
hot. And hot it did become. Running down
with a strong ebb tide through the Smith's
inlet channel, we suddenly found a gunboat in
the middle of the channel on the bar. It was
too late to stop, so we put her at it, almost
grazing the gunboat's sides and receiving her
broadside point blank. Mrs. Randolph had
retired to her place of safety, but she told me
afterwards that, alarmed as she was, she could
not help laughing when, after she had been
there only an instant, my coloured servant, who
had evidently fixed upon the place as appearing
to be the most safe, jumped right on the top of
her, his teeth chattering through fear. How

we laughed the next morning, and how poor
Sam got chaffed, but he became quite a cool
hand, and when we were running in, in daylight,
in the *Will-o-the-Wisp* (as I have already re-
lated), and the shot were coming thick, Sam
appeared upon the bridge with his usual
" Coffee Sar ! "

After we had got rid of our friend on the
bar, we were heavily peppered by her consorts
outside, from whom we received no damage,
but we fell in with very bad weather, and the
ship was under water most of the time. Right
glad I was to land my passengers, who were
half dead through sea-sickness, exposure, and
fatigue.

Although it was a hard trip it paid well, as
we had on board coming out a most magnificent cargo, a great deal of it Sea Island
cotton, the profit upon which and the provisions
I had taken in amounted to over £85,000—
not bad work for about twenty days !

CHAPTER XI

HAVANA AND GALVESTON

HAVANA was a great blockade-running centre to and from the Gulf ports, but until Wilmington was closed I did not attempt to utilise it, for many reasons preferring Nassau and the last named port. I went over there, however, several times, partly on business, and partly on pleasure, and a lovely city it was. Cuba was then in the heyday of success, and no one who had not visited its capital could have imagined that such a

L

gay and beautiful city existed in the West
Indies. Money seemed no object. And
fortunately there was plenty, for everything
was extravagantly dear, and I should think
that at that time it was one of the most if not
the most expensive city in the world to
live in.

To us blockade-runners, accustomed to the
hard life in the South and the contracted
surroundings of Nassau, Havana appeared
like Paradise; good hotels and casinos, a
capital theatre, magnificent equipages, military
bands, handsome women, and, last but not
least, the lavish and genial hospitality dis-
pensed by our Consul-General, Mr. Crawford,
and his charming daughters at their house,
" Buenos Ayres," made a residence in Havana
like a rest in an oasis to the weary traveller
of the desert. But it was not all pleasure,
as far as I was concerned. I had my business
with its anxieties to attend to, and on one of
my visits I had a rather adventurous trip to
Nassau in a small schooner which I had
chartered to convey some boiler tubes there.
Being very anxious to reach Nassau quickly,

I decided to go in her instead of waiting for
the mail steamer which left a few days later.

I made a start in the small craft (her size
can be imagined when I state that she was
a man-of-war's pinnace raised upon) manned
by nine niggers. The first day out we encountered a furious gale in the Gulf-stream,
and it is a marvel our little craft lived
through it, for a fearful sea was running.
However, she proved an excellent sea-boat,
and when the gale subsided we found ourselves on the Bahama banks becalmed; for
nine days we drifted helplessly over them,
suffering agonies from the heat, hunger, and
thirst, as we had only laid in provisions for
about four days, and to make matters worse
the bung had been left out of our fresh-
water cask and in the gale the water was
rendered undrinkable by the salt water washing
over it. Fortunately I had laid in a supply of
a dozen of claret and a dozen of beer, and
this was all we had to divide between us;
however, everything has an end, and on the
ninth day we had a spanking breeze which
carried us in to Nassau, but not until we had

been passed about twenty miles outside by
the mail steamer in which I could have come,
and whose captain, recognising me on board
the schooner, jeered at me from his bridge.

When Wilmington was on the point of
falling there was nothing for it but to transfer
our operations to Galveston, and to accomplish
this I took the *Banshee* No. 2 over to Havana
with a valuable cargo, accompanied by Frank
Hurst, in order to make an attempt to run
into Galveston : this proved to be my last
trip, but it was far from being the least
exciting. When all was ready we experienced
the greatest difficulty in finding a Galveston
pilot. Though, owing to the high rate of
pay, numbers of men were to be found ready
to offer their services, it was extremely hard
to obtain competent men. After considerable
delay we had to content ourselves at last
with a man who *said* he knew all about the
port, but who turned out to be absolutely
worthless. We then made a start, and with
the exception of meeting with the most
violent thunderstorm, in which the lightning
was something awful, nothing extraordinary

occurred on our passage across the Gulf of
Mexico, and we scarcely saw a sail—very
different from our experiences between Nassau
and Wilmington, when it was generally a case
of "sail on the port bow" or "steamer right
ahead" at all hours of the day.

The third evening after leaving Havana
we had run our distance, and, on heaving the
lead and finding that we were within a few
miles of the shore, we steamed cautiously on
in order to try and make out the blockading
squadron or the land. It was a comparatively
calm and very dark night, just the one for
the purpose, but within an hour all had
changed and it commenced to blow a regular
" Norther," a wind which is very prevalent on
that coast. Until then I had no idea what
a " Norther" meant; first rain came down in
torrents, then out of the inky blackness of
clouds and rain came furious gusts, until a
hurricane was blowing against which, notwithstanding that we were steaming at full speed,
we made little or no way, and although the
sea was smooth our decks were swept by
white foam and spray. Suddenly we made

out some dark objects all round us, and found ourselves drifting helplessly among the ships of the blockading squadron, which were steaming hard to their anchors, and at one moment we were almost jostling two of them ; whether they knew what we were, or mistook us for one of themselves matters not ; they were too much occupied about their own safety to attempt to interfere.

As to attempt to get into Galveston that night would have been madness, we let the *Banshee* drift and, when we thought we were clear of the fleet, we steamed slowly seaward, after a while shaping a course so as to make the land about thirty miles to the south-west at daylight. We succeeded in doing this and quietly dropped our anchor in perfectly calm water, the " Norther " having subsided almost as quickly as it had risen. Having seen enough of our pilot to realise that he was no good whatever, we decided after a conference to lie all day where we were, keeping a sharp look - out and steam handy, and determined as evening came on to creep slowly up the coast until we made out the blockading fleet, then to anchor again and make a bold dash at daylight for our port.

All went well; we were unmolested during the day and got under weigh towards evening, passing close to a wreck which we recognised as our old friend the *Will-o'-the-Wisp*, which had been driven ashore and lost on the very first trip she made after I had sold her. Immediately afterwards we very nearly lost our own ship too. Seeing a post of Confederate soldiers close by on the beach, we determined to steam close in and communicate with them in order to learn all about the tactics of the blockaders and our exact distance from Galveston. We backed her close in to the breakers in order to speak, but when the order was given to go ahead she declined to move, and the chief engineer reported that something had gone wrong with the cylinder valve, and that she must heave to for repairs. It was an anxious moment; the *Banshee* had barely three fathoms beneath her, and her stern was almost in the white water. We let go the anchor, but in the heavy swell it failed to hold: the pilot was in a helpless state of flurry when he found that we were drifting slowly but steadily towards the shore, but Steele's presence of mind never for one moment deserted him. The comparatively few minutes which occupied the engineers in temporarily remedying the defect seemed like hours in the presence of the danger momentarily threatening us. When, at length, the engineers managed to turn her ahead we on the bridge were greatly relieved to see her point seawards and clear the breakers. I have often thought since, if a disaster had happened and we had lost the ship, how stupid we should have been thought by people at home.

As soon as we reached deep water the damage was permanently repaired, and we steamed cautiously up the coast, until about sundown we made out the topmasts of the blockading squadron right ahead. We promptly stopped, calculating that, as they were about ten to eleven miles from us, Galveston must lie a little further on our port bow. We let go our anchor and prepared for an anxious night; all hands were on deck and the cable

was ready to be unshackled at a moment's
notice, with steam as nearly ready as possible
without blowing off, as at any moment a
prowler from the squadron patrolling the coast
might have made us out. We had not been
lying thus very long when suddenly on the
starboard bow we made out a cruiser steaming
towards us evidently on the prowl. It was
a critical time ; all hands were on deck, a man
standing by to knock the shackle out of the
chain cable, and the engineers at their stations.
Thanks to the backing of the coast, our friend
did not discover us and to our relief disappeared to the southward.

After this all was quiet during the re-
mainder of the night, which, fortunately for
us, was very dark, and about two hours before
daylight we quietly raised our anchor and
steamed slowly on, feeling our way cautiously
by the lead, and hoping, when daylight fairly
broke, to find ourselves inside the fleet
opposite Galveston and able to make a short
dash for the bar. We had been under weigh
some time, when suddenly we discovered a
launch close to us on the port bow filled with

Northern blue-jackets and marines. "Full speed ahead," shouted Steele, and we were within an ace of running her down as we almost grazed her with our port paddle-wheel. Hurst and I looked straight down into the boat, waving them a parting salute. The crew seemed only too thankful at their narrow escape to open fire, but they soon regained their senses and threw up rocket after rocket in our wake as a warning to the blockading fleet to be on the alert.

Daylight was then slowly breaking, and the first thing we discovered was that we had not taken sufficient account of the effects of the "Norther" on the current; instead of being opposite the town with the fleet broad on to our starboard beam, we found ourselves down three or four miles from it and the most leeward blockader close to us on our bow. It was a moment for immediate decision: the alternatives were to turn tail and stand a chase to seaward by their fastest cruisers with chance of capture, and in any case a return to Havana as we had not sufficient coal for another attempt, or to make a dash for it and

take the fire of the squadron. In an instant
we decided to go for it, and orders to turn
ahead full speed were given; but the difficulty
now to be overcome was that we could not
make for the main channel without going
through the fleet. This would have been
certain destruction, so we had to make for
a sort of swash channel along the beach,
which, however, was nothing but a *cul-de-sac*,
and to get from it into the main channel.
Shoal water and heavy breakers had to be
passed, but there was now no other choice
open to us.

By this time the fleet had opened fire upon
us, and shells were bursting merrily around
as we took the fire of each ship which we
passed. Fortunately there was a narrow
shoal between us, which prevented them from
approaching within about half a mile of us;
luckily also for us they were in rough water
on the windward side of the shoal and could
not lay their guns with precision. And to
this we owed our escape, as, although our
funnels were riddled with shell splinters, we
received no damage and had only one man

wounded. But the worst was to come; we
saw the white water already ahead, and we
knew our only chance was to bump through
it, being well aware that if she stuck fast we
should lose the ship and all our lives, for no
boat, even if it could have been launched,
would have lived in such a surf.

With two leadsmen in the chains we
approached our fate, taking no notice of the
bursting shells and round shot to which the
blockaders treated us in their desperation;
it was not a question of the fathoms but of the
feet we were drawing: twelve feet, ten, nine,
and when we put her at it, as you do a horse
at a jump, and as her nose was entering the
white water, "eight feet" was sung out. A
moment afterwards we touched and hung;
and I thought all was over, when a big wave
came rolling along and lifted our stern and
the ship bodily with a crack which could be
heard a quarter of a mile off, and which we
thought meant that her back was broken.

She once more went ahead: the worst was
over, and, after two or three minor bumps, we
were in the deep channel, helm hard a-star-

E.A.S.H.E.E No. 2. RUNNING THE GAUNTLET OF THE GALVESTON BLOCKADING SQUADRON IN DAYLIGHT.

To face page 156.

board and heading for Galveston Bay, leaving
the disappointed blockaders astern. It was a
reckless undertaking and a narrow escape, but
we were safe in, and after an examination by
the health officer we steamed gaily up to the
town, the wharves of which were crowded by
people, who, gazing to seaward, had watched
our exploit with much interest, and who
cheered us heartily upon its success.

I found Galveston a most forsaken place;
its streets covered with sand, its wharves
rotting, its defences in a most deplorable
condition, very different from those at Wilmington, and if the Northerners had taken
the trouble I think that they could easily
have possessed themselves of it. But our
welcome was warm, and during the *Banshee's*
long stay we had a real good time; General
Magruder was in command, and many a
cheery entertainment we had on board with
him and his staff as guests, who were all
musical. We had a capital French cook, and
as plenty of game, fish, and oysters were
procurable, and our good liquor was plentiful,
we had all the necessary ingredients for many

most sociable evenings—this was the bright
side of the picture.

The reverse was the difficulty I had in
procuring a suitable outward cargo; the inward one was all right, and I found our
assortment would sell well, but the trouble
was to obtain cotton: there was extremely
little of it left near the seaboard, and to
get it from further up country was a long,
tedious, and expensive process. Moreover,
I found there would be great difficulty in
having it pressed, and to take a cargo of
half-pressed cotton meant very serious loss
indeed; however, having arranged for the
sale by auction of the inward cargo, Hurst
and I started for Houston, the capital of
Texas, armed with a letter of introduction
to the most influential merchant there, who
agreed after endless negotiations to provide
at a high price a full-pressed cargo, but
required a long time for delivery and pay-
ment half in Confederate money (being part
of the proceeds of our inward cargo), and
the balance by drafts on home. This meant
a further loss in withdrawing my superfluous

proceeds from the country, but as no better bargain could be made I agreed.

Houston, in those days, was a pretty little town, very dull of course, but fortunately we made the acquaintance of a charming family, refugees from Baton Rouge, who were most kind to us, and I shall ever feel grateful to Mrs. Avery and her fair daughters for the hospitality which they extended to me.

After concluding these arrangements I returned to Galveston, being rather amused on the journey by the sudden stoppage of the train, which had been crawling along at about ten miles an hour, followed by the leisurely exit of the conductor and engine driver each with a gun on his shoulder, who calmly disappeared across the prairie on a gunning expedition. After about an hour's delay the sportsmen returned fairly successful, and with "all aboard" we resumed our journey.

A few days subsequently I witnessed a sad sight—the execution of a deserter, a fine fellow, sergeant of artillery, whose only offence was that he had crossed the Mississippi into the Northern lines in order to visit his wife and family, intending, it was believed, to return ; he was captured, however, and condemned to death by court - martial, and the whole of the garrison of Galveston was paraded to witness his execution. It was an anxious time for the authorities, as it was expected that his battery would attempt a rescue, so the other two batteries were drawn up opposite with guns loaded ready to fire on it if it did. The sergeant was led out, and six men were placed a few paces in front of him ; after refusing to have his eyes bandaged, he dropped his hand as a signal for them to fire ; a report as from one rifle rang out, and he dropped on his face dead. The saddest part of this incident was, that within an hour of his execution a pardon arrived from head-quarters at Houston on a railway trolly ; no locomotive being available four men had worked the trolly down, but too late.

Finding that the accumulation of cargo and consequent loading of the *Banshee* would occupy a long time, and owing to the critical state of affairs in the South rendering it abso-lutely necessary for me to return to Nassau

as soon as possible, I decided to take a passage
in a friend's blockade-runner then ready to
start, leaving my able lieutenant Frank Hurst to
settle up things and come out in the *Banshee*.
But I did not like it at all; it was the first
time I was to try the venture in a strange
craft and as a mere passenger, and from what
I had seen of the skipper I had not over
much confidence in him.

On a night which was eminently suited for
the purpose we made a start, but no sooner did
we get down to the Tripod, which marked the
entrance to the channel, than we made out
a couple of the blockaders — a sight quite
enough for the nerves of our captain, who
declared we should certainly be seen and
immediately gave orders to turn back. This
was not my idea of blockade-running as I
had been accustomed to it, but being a passenger I had no *locus standi* on board; we put
back to the harbour and next morning were
well chaffed. To make a long story short
we made a second attempt next night with
like results, and I was beginning to feel
thoroughly disgusted. Every hour's delay

M

with a growing moon now increased our risks ;
on the third night, by dint of goading the
skipper, whose coal was running short, I
persuaded him to harden his heart and make
a run for it. When we reached the Tripod
we made out several of the squadron, but we
put our helm a-starboard, ran along the land,
and fortunately got clear.

Crossing the Gulf of Mexico we made out
nothing ; perhaps this was because no look-out
was kept ; and mightily glad I was when we
made the coast of Cuba and steamed into
Havana. This trip was certainly a revelation
to me as regards blockade-running, and no
wonder many a fine boat, navigated, no doubt,
on the same lines as the —— had been thrown
away.

This was my last trip, the twenty-eighth—
a record, I think, for any Englishman during
the war, and considering the narrow squeaks
that I had, and that I only came to grief once
in the *Night Hawk*, I had a great deal to be
thankful for.

Upon my arrival in Havana I found the
mail boat was starting for Nassau next day,

and in her I took my passage. I found Nassau
much changed, as during my absence Wilmington, after an heroic defence of Fort Fisher
by my old friend Lamb, had been captured,
and had it not been for the supineness (not to
use a stronger phrase) of General Bragg, who
commanded the Confederate forces outside the
fort and who failed to attack the Northern
attacking force in the rear when the assault
was made, Lamb's second defence would have
been as successful as the first, and Fort Fisher
and Wilmington would have been saved to
the Confederate Government—a result which
might have had a very important bearing upon
the issue of the struggle. Wilmington and
Charleston being now closed, Nassau's days
as a blockade-running centre were over, and
the only thing to do was to wind up our affairs
as well as we could, and prepare to go home.
Even then it was evident that the game was
up as far as the South was concerned, and
very shortly afterwards we heard of Lee's
surrender and the virtual ending of the war.

In the interim the *Banshee* arrived, having
cleared out of Galveston without trouble and

transhipped her cargo at Havana, which, although the war was over, sold for very high prices in Liverpool. But the liquidation of our affairs generally was a disastrous one; our steamers were practically valueless; and as a matter of fact the *Banshee* and *Night Hawk*, which I sent home, and which had cost between them some £70,000, we sold for £6000; two or three other boats which I sent to South America for sale realised miserable prices, so that this, combined with the enormous stakes we had imprisoned in the South, and which were confiscated, took the gilt considerably off our gingerbread.

It had been an exciting and eventful period, however, and had I gone through it again with the experience I had gained in the trade, I could have made large fortunes for my employers and myself; but in the early part of the war, when the Northerners owing to want of ships could only blockade the Southern ports in a half-hearted way, we let our golden opportunity slip in trying to work with indifferent tools, *i.e.* slow, worn-out, heavy-draught steamers, and it was not until almost too late that my friends at home woke up and sent me out a better class of boat. By that time the blockade had become most stringent, and to evade it was an affair involving a tremendous risk, even with the fastest and best equipped vessels and commanded by the most daring men.

After closing up my affairs in Nassau I returned home for, what I think I deserved, a well-earned rest; and I am sure I needed it, as the hard life I had led, combined with the after effects of yellow fever and fever and ague, had played havoc with my nervous system. This trouble quiet life in England soon put right, and in a few months I found myself bound for India as a partner in the house in Bombay, with quite a different life to look forward to, but very pleasant recollections of the experience I had gained and the good friends I had made. The death rate, however, among those friends has lately been heavy, and there are very few left (I think, sad to relate, Murray-Aynsley and Frank Hurst now only remain) of the good comrades, who would always have stood by each other in any difficulty or danger.

CHAPTER XII

BLOCKADES OF THE PAST AND THE FUTURE

Present compared with past conditions—Lessons of former blockades—
Plan of the Northern States—Action of the Gulf-stream—Search-
lights; their value to blockaders and blockaded—Quick-firing
guns—Speed of modern ships as affecting a blockade—National
character—Battle-ships and cruisers.

ALTHOUGH it is extremely improbable that the
world will ever again witness a war carried
on under conditions similar to those obtaining in the contest carried on between the
North and South in the sixties, still it is
possible, as recent events have shown, that the
United States might find themselves involved
in a struggle with a first-rate maritime Power.
If this were the case, the first step to be taken
by that Power would be to blockade the United
States ports. This being so, it is interesting
to consider how, owing to increased speed,
quick-firing guns, and search-lights, the re-

lationships between blockaders and blockade-runners have been affected during the last thirty years.

In the civil war the conditions were very different from those likely to occur in the future ; the blockade-runners of those days were unarmed, and their business was to dodge, not to fight, the blockaders, and the shortness of the run before a safe port could be reached made possible a heavy outlay for building and maintaining special vessels. But to my mind the most salient alteration in the conditions affecting the question is the intro-duction of quick-firing guns, search-lights, and increased speed.

Before considering the effect of these changes on the future of blockading, it will be as well to ascertain what lessons were learnt from the blockade of the American coast.

We soon discovered that with due care and pluck the risk was far less than people believed; except in a few cases our losses were caused by ignorance of position in making the port.   In some cases this was owing to the fact of our being chased about by day ; in others it was

caused by the irregular action of the Gulf-
stream ; and in some cases it was due to
neglect and want of care in keeping a proper
look-out at daylight; also to not keeping
clear of vessels when seen, and to steaming
too fast when not necessary, thereby causing
smoke, which discovered to the blockaders the
position of the runner. Discovery (after taking
all possible precautions) by a faster vessel was
the cause of a small minority of captures.

Again, the blockade was carried on on
a wrong principle. The Northern plan was,
—to keep a number of ships close off the
port, as a rule anchoring by day and by
night moving close in, and a few ships at
a moderate distance from the land. This
plan enabled runners to lie out a fair distance
from the shore at sunset so as to run in when
the time came, having the whole night before
them should they be seen. On coming out,
we felt that after the first ten miles or so from
the shore there was little chance of anything
seeing us before daylight, and if we were seen
then the inshore squadron could not join in the
chase.

Off Bermuda I rarely saw a cruiser; off the Bahamas there were three or four, but not well placed; at sea most of the cruisers were in pairs, as far as I could make out; so that their limit of vision was only that of one, and in such a case there is always the possibility of the one trusting to the other to keep a good look-out.

The action of the Gulf-stream was an important factor in the calculations which the blockade-runners had to take into consideration. Its rate is so uncertain, that unless you had taken a sight the day before you got in you could not depend upon your position, and although it could be verified by the soundings it could not be laid down by them alone. Star observation, from the uncertain horizon, could not be depended upon, and the moon of course was not available; on the other hand, the general haze was in our favour.

That in the future there will ever be a similar blockade is improbable; it will be one of armed ships against armed ships, and the only exception, if it can be called running a blockade, will be that of armed merchant-ships bringing food to England, which will be required to meet cruisers on the open sea, and not to run in and out of a blockaded port.

I will now take up the three points of speed, quick-firing guns, and search-lights.

To begin with search-lights : on first thoughts the search-light would appear to be a formidable weapon in the hands of the blockader ; but on consideration I don't think it is so, excepting perhaps in the case of a runner being chased at night, or into the night, by a cruiser of equal or superior speed which could, by means of her search - light, keep her quarry under observation, and, if within range, perhaps speedily sink her. In the dash through an inside squadron lying off a port this would not apply. True, it would be very uncomfortable for the blockade-runner to find herself within the sphere of a dozen search-lights all around her, but it would be equally uncomfortable for the ships exhibiting those lights were they within range of the protecting fort, as they would most probably immediately be plugged by its guns. Moreover, a fort supplied with search-lights could be constantly flashing them over the area comprised within the range of its guns, and this would tend to force a blockading fleet to keep at a more respectable distance and so widen out and render the passage between its lines more easy for the blockade-runner.

The introduction of the search-light therefore appears to me to be in favour of the runner. I assume that the light is in use at the port from which the runner starts and is protected by guns. As most likely it will be at fixed points, and as there can be no object for secrecy in its use, it can be flashed from time to time irregularly so as to show whether the vicinity of the port is clear of hostile cruisers or not. No cruiser will care to come within range of the light; consequently the runner will have the advantage of seeing his road is clear before him when he starts, and the further out the cruisers are, the further apart, given equal numbers, must they be.

On the other hand, the blockader wishes to keep his position dark and will not use his light for fear of being seen; so it is useless to him. Again, a light on the Mound at Fort

Fisher would have been invaluable to us; the
light thrown up into the air would have been
of no use to the blockader, while to us it would
have fixed the position and enabled us to run
in with confidence.   For my part, if in command of a blockader, unless it was to call
friends to my assistance, I would prefer not
to use the light.

The present condition of affairs with regard
to quick-firing guns and the armament of
modern war-vessels, in my opinion, would
be distinctly in favour of the blockader.
Seeing how many more of this description
of gun are carried by our modern ships
compared with the slow-firing old-fashioned
guns of thirty years ago, to say nothing of
their increased range and accuracy, I fear a
blockade-runner would stand a poor chance if
she allowed herself to come within the range
of the guns of a cruiser so armed, at all events
in daylight.   Of course at night, and if she
were within the range of the guns of a protecting fort, her chances would be more
equally balanced; as the fort would be
supplied with similar guns to those of her

assailants, and would doubtless use them with effect. I am of the opinion, therefore, that the modern gun is distinctly in favour of the blockader as compared with the runner. The report of the quick-firing gun is much sharper and the flash much more brilliant than that of the old-fashioned gun ; and this constitutes an additional element in favour of the blockader, for the report and flash, being heard and seen at a greater distance, would call any neigh-bouring cruiser to the blockader's assistance.

Though the increase of speed attained by modern ships affects both sides, the enormous speed now developed by cruisers and torpedo destroyers would seem at first sight to give the blockading force a distinct advantage. But if war-vessels have improved their speed merchant-steamers have done the same ; and, as I have pointed out in previous chapters, the blockade-runner has several points in her favour by always being in good going condition and on the alert, whereas the blockader cannot always have steam handy or be ready for the advent of the runner on the scene. If, how-ever, the maritime Power in question could afford a large number of exceedingly fast cruisers and torpedo catchers to be constantly patrolling the seas adjacent to the blockaded ports, and could keep those vessels supplied with coals, I think the runner's chances of success would be materially reduced under the new regime. But could this be done, seeing the difficulty there would be of procuring coal and supplies from perhaps a distant base? There is one factor resulting from increased speed which certainly is in favour of the runner; that is, in consequence of her being at sea a shorter time while making her hazardous passage, her risk is diminished. And this is a material point. In the olden days it was considered a fast passage if the distance between Wilmington and Nassau, which now could be traversed in some thirty hours, was covered in fifty. On the whole, therefore, increased speed is in favour of the runner. Speed requires coal, and a man who knows what he has to do can economise coal to an extent unattainable by the man whose movements are uncertain. He can be either going full speed with clear fires, or be ready for it to a greater extent than a man who is waiting until his speed is required. As probably in the future there will not be short runs from shallow ports, the runner can be of a size equal to, if not greater than, the blockader; consequently, unless in smooth water, more likely to attain greater speed.

A point of great importance, which should not be overlooked, is the effect of national character. In the American war, with the exception of one or two Danes, all the officers and crews of the runners were either British or Southerners. It is a question whether any other European State would show sufficient spirit of enterprise to carry a blockade on a large scale to a successful issue. What is wanted in blockade-runners is not only capable leaders, but a large number of people who will trust each other and their leaders.

Hitherto I have only considered the question of evading a superior force outside, and of being prepared to run and not to fight unless necessary. A fleet, if going to sea, ought to go by day and fight its way out. A squadron of cruisers, on the other hand, may

find it advisable to slip out night by night
and meet at a given distant rendezvous, at
the same time being prepared to act on their
own individual account if necessary; *i.e.* if
they find that the chance of the original plan
cannot be carried out. Ships of the line of
battle cannot do this. They must in all
probability fight together or fail, as their not
being able to come out without fighting shows
that there is a fleet of battle ships outside. If
equal powers are inside and out, I do not
think that any blockade can be made effective ;
the chances of breaking a modern blockade
compared with those which existed in the
sixties are much the same, provided the runner
has the proper tools to work with, in the shape
of speedy and seaworthy steamers commanded
and manned by determined and cautious men.

INDEX

N

THE END

Printed by R. & R. CLARK, LIMITED, *Edinburgh*

O C E A N

25

D

TROPIC OF CANCER

20

lvador or
I A

M

A

Turk I.

S

G.
magua I.

Anguilla I.

P. de Maysi

Magna Channel

SAN JUAN

Virgin I.

I. S.t Martin

Edward Channel

Tortuga I.

Domingo

C. Samana

PUERTO RICO

St Thomas

Santa Cruz

Cap Haytien

S.t DOMINGO

HAITI

Cavarel

SAN DOMINGO

ria

PORT AU PRINCE

C. Beata

70°

65°

THE END

Printed by R. & R. CLARK, LIMITED, *Edinburgh*

London: John Murray.

www.ingramcontent.com/pod-product-compliance
Lightning Source LLC
Chambersburg PA
CBHW020608030726
47497CB00007B/2141